---- ★ ----

That morning, along with the usual assortment of bills, letters and Victoria's Secret catalogs, I received a large envelope. It was brown, nine by twelve, and it was addressed with letters cut from a magazine. At first, I thought it was a joke and I laughed as I opened the envelope. Inside was a glossy back-and-white photograph—a photograph of me doing something I never realized anyone had witnessed. I was standing outside Abe Parson's store, picking up a yellow maple leaf. By itself, the photo didn't strike me as particularly threatening. But the note did. It, too, was fashioned from magazine letters and the message was short and simple: *STiLL aLIve?*

---- ★ ----

Previously published Worldwide Mystery title by
KATHLEEN ANNE BARRETT

MILWAUKEE SUMMERS CAN BE DEADLY

Milwaukee

Autumns Can Be

LETHAL

Kathleen Anne Barrett

WORLDWIDE.

TORONTO • NEW YORK • LONDON
AMSTERDAM • PARIS • SYDNEY • HAMBURG
STOCKHOLM • ATHENS • TOKYO • MILAN
MADRID • WARSAW • BUDAPEST • AUCKLAND

To Winifred Chor (1928-1995)

MILWAUKEE AUTUMNS CAN BE LETHAL

A Worldwide Mystery/October 2001

First published by Thomas Bouregy & Company, Inc.

ISBN 0-373-26399-6

Printed in U.S.A.

Acknowledgments

I wish to acknowledge and thank the following people for their special efforts in helping me complete this book: My father, Dr. James M. Barrett; my friend Debra Wojtowski; and my cousin-in-law, Donna Zahorik.

PROLOGUE

I STILL CAN'T GET OVER how difficult my third murder investigation was. I was totally surprised by the solution and throughout most of it, I was followed almost everywhere I went. I'm sure I don't have to tell you how terrifying that was. And those letters and photographs. To this day, I get a knot in my stomach just at the sight of a nine-by-twelve-inch envelope.

My name is Beth Hartley, by the way. I'm forty-three years old, divorced from my first husband and widowed from my second (no children, I'm sorry to say). I live on the east side of Milwaukee in an enormous and really cool house I inherited six years ago from my Aunt Sarah. She also left me all of her antiques and a whole ton of money. And one of the best parts of all is that her housekeeper, Mrs. Gunther, whom I've known all my life, comes in every Monday, Wednesday, and Friday and I never really have to do a thing. Now tell me that isn't a dream come true.

I'm a lawyer but I thoroughly hated it so I quit, took my secretary, Janice Grezinski, with me, and started my own business doing legal research and writing for other lawyers. A few years later, I hired Emily Schaeffer, also a lawyer, whom I've known since the fifth grade. Just recently, Mike Shepard, a very close friend who went to law school and undergrad with me, also joined our little group because we had too much to do and I was sick and tired of working so hard. I run the business out of my house (in the library) and when we need to do research we either use Lexis, a computer legal research tool, or go to the Marquette University Law Library. It's a really wonderful way to make a living and we're totally laid back and informal so there's hardly ever any tension except when I'm trying to solve a murder.

It was fall, my favorite season, and I was feeling that excited expectation I've always associated with the beginning of a school year. The air was clean and crisp, the grass a lush, rich green, and autumn leaves were flitting and floating against a deep blue sky. I was gazing out my kitchen window one Friday afternoon as a bright yellow bus let off a group of schoolchildren, the girls dressed in navy-and-green plaid jumpers with white blouses, the boys in green slacks, white shirts, and navy monogrammed cardigans. I was so jealous. I was right in the midst of my nostalgic reverie when I got a phone call from an old friend from law school named Don Balstrum. He had opened his own family law practice right after graduation with another one of our classmates, a guy named Glen Nolte. He'd accepted a personal injury case from one of his divorce clients (normally, he only did divorces), needed to file a motion for summary judgment, and didn't have the time or the inclination to write the brief.

"Beth, how ya doin'?" Don said when I took the call. "It's Don Balstrum."

I hesitated because I couldn't place him at first.

"From law school?" he said.

"Hey, how are you?" I said. "How's the practice?"

"Great, just great, but I have a small matter I think you might be able to help me with."

He told me about Lana Shaw (he called her Laney), the divorce client and close friend he said literally begged him to represent her on a personal injury claim despite his lack of experience in the area. Don was about to go to trial on one of his divorce cases and had absolutely no time to spare. I agreed to write the brief for him and that's when big trouble began.

ONE

IT WAS TUESDAY, OCTOBER 13—about two and a half weeks after I'd met with Don at his office—and we'd agreed that I would deliver his brief that evening at around eight o'clock (he worked late every night and promised he'd be there). I was finished a little early and I was on my way shortly before seven. The office was on Wells Street, a few blocks west of the Milwaukee River, so it took me only minutes to get there. The front door of the building was unlocked when I arrived. I walked up the stairs, expecting to hear voices or some sign of occupancy, but everything was silent. When I entered the law office suite, I could hear a fax machine working in the back room and the buzzing of fluorescent lights. Nothing else.

I walked on back and peeked in the copy room. The copy machine was on, giving off a faint buzz almost masked by the sound of a fax coming through. A copy of a complaint was in the tray, the original on top of the machine. I went over to the fax machine and studied the incoming document. It was a set of answers to interrogatories—a bunch of questions asked by one party to a lawsuit of another—nearly all of which were unanswered and objected to as being either too vague, too broad, or unlikely to lead to the discovery of admissible evidence. (This is one of those little games lawyers play just to get on one another's nerves.)

I walked toward Don's office, passing Glen Nolte's on the way. Glen's light was off but I could still see his desk, neat as could be, everything in perfectly aligned little piles. I used to work with a guy who had a desk like that. He always had two piles of papers, very neatly stacked. One was full of missed deadlines. The other was full of deadlines that would be missed by the time he got to them.

Don's door, the next one down, was open and the light was on. I tiptoed to the doorway and peeked around the corner. Don was there, seated at his desk, looking pretty much the same as the last time I'd seen him—except for the ghastly hole in the side of his head. I sucked in my breath and my eyes filled with tears.

"Oh, no," I said. "Oh, my gosh." I felt a wave of nausea wash over me and I sat on the edge of the couch across from his desk. For a moment, I actually thought of trying to help him, which was utterly ridiculous. I was about as sure as I could be that he was dead and that the cause of death was a gunshot wound to his head. For all I knew, the person who'd fired the shot was still somewhere in the building. Staying right where I was seemed like the most prudent thing to do, so I picked up the phone and dialed 911.

Twenty minutes later, Brian McHenry (an old grade-school friend who is now a Milwaukee homicide detective and an on-again-off-again questionably significant other) came through the door with an entourage of cops and assorted investigator types.

He pursed his lips and gave me a lingering look of extreme irritation. "Beth," he said in a flat tone. "Are we at it again?"

I pursed my lips right back, only I did a much better job of it. "Are we at what again?" I said in a testy voice.

He took in a breath, let it out, and looked away. "Roberson," he said in the direction of a young woman, and she turned around. "Find an empty office and get a statement from Hartley here." He waved his hand in my direction without looking at me. She looked at his face and then at mine, then back at his. "Yes, sir," she said quietly.

I showed her to Glen Nolte's office, turned on the light, and sat down behind his desk, all of which appeared to unnerve her a bit. She couldn't have been more than twenty-five, with pale, peachy skin, soft blond curls worn short around her face, and a slight build, about five-two or five-three. She took a seat on the other side of the desk and studied my face.

"Are you acquainted with the deceased?" she asked.

I told her the whole story as she took careful notes, and about five minutes later, Brian came back.

"Have you finished here?" he asked Ms. Roberson.

She gave him a coy little smile and said, "Yes, sir."

Brian nodded and blushed almost imperceptibly, but I knew him well enough to have noticed. "I'll take over from here," he said, and she got up and left.

I stared at him, waiting for him to speak. He walked around the room, gave everything in it a cursory glance, and looked back at me. "What are you doing here, Beth?"

I closed my eyes and sighed. "Brian, I know this guy from law school. I was doing a brief for him. I told him I'd deliver it personally by eight o'clock tonight and that's what I was doing. Except I was early and when I got here he was dead."

"How did you get in?" he asked.

"The doors were unlocked. I just walked right in. He knew I was coming. I called ahead and left a message on his voice mail."

Brian lifted his head and frowned. "What time?" he said.

I thought for a moment. "It had to be around a quarter to seven," I said. "Maybe five minutes later."

Brian nodded and gazed out Glen's window. Then he looked back at me and pursed his lips again. "I suppose you're going to feel a special obligation to get involved in the investigation, now. Am I right?'' he said.

I gave him a thoughtful look. "Well...now that you mention it, I suppose I really should."

Brian's face turned a deep purplish-red. He swallowed hard and walked out the door, just like that. This is typical behavior on his part. For some reason I cannot fathom, he believes that I am interfering with his job.

"YOU FOUND his body?'' Mike Shepard nearly screeched when I told him about it early the next morning. He sat on the edge of one of my kitchen chairs and stared at me. "Do they have any leads?"

"Not that I know of," I said. "Not that Brian would ever consider sharing them with me if they did."

Mike gave me a comprehending look. He knows all about Brian and me, and Brian's inability to accept the fact that I solved two of Milwaukee's recent murders without any help from the police (well, almost). Mrs. Gunther refers to him as That Homicide Detective whenever he's in one of his obnoxious moods.

Mike squinted at me. "Who do you think did it?"

"How should I know?" I said with a laugh.

"Come on, you can't tell me you haven't started those investigative wheels turning inside that little head of yours," he said with a mischievous smirk.

I gave him a lopsided smile. "Well, I'll tell you

one thing," I said. "Even if I wouldn't have thought of getting involved before, I'm definitely going to do it now after the hard time Brian gave me last night."

Mike made a fist and raised it skyward. "Yes!" he said with a grin. Then he looked at me with undisguised expectation. "How would you like some help this time?"

I wrinkled my brow. "From whom?"

He sighed loudly and *very* melodramatically, then just sat there and stared at me.

I stared back and waited. It drives me nuts when he does that, and he does it all the time.

"From *me*," he finally said, his face tinting a light shade of pink.

I thought about it for a few moments and then grinned at him. "Okay," I said. "Let's do it."

"Let's do what?" Emily said when she and Janice came into the kitchen. As you may already know, Emily has never been too keen on my murder investigating hobby, either. No sense of adventure, Janice says. Just another case of jealousy, according to Mike.

"I'll let you handle this one," Mike said.

"Thanks a lot," I mumbled. Both Emily and Janice were frowning at me. I took a moment and decided to just get it over with.

"The guy I was doing that brief for got murdered yesterday so Mike and I are going to try to solve the murder." I made one of those shoulder-shrugging, palm-opening, So-what's-the-big-deal? sort of gestures.

Emily gave me a strained smile, said absolutely nothing, and went to the cupboard for a coffee mug. I arched my brows as she walked by and Janice gave me a little shrug. Janice, by the way, is how I got involved in this business to begin with. Her younger brother's murder was the first one I solved.

After Em, Janice, and Mike went into the library, my housekeeper, Mrs. Gunther, arrived. I gave her a teasing grin and said, "Guess what?"

She looked at me askance and raised one bushy eyebrow.

"I'm going to try to solve another murder," I said.

She put her hands on her hips and scowled with a smile sneaking through.

"Just wanted to let you know," I said, and went to the library myself.

I pulled out Don's file (the one for the brief he'd assigned me) and started to page through it. I stopped when I got to the notes I'd taken about the client who had brought the suit. Laney Shaw. She was a good friend, Don had said. No, I think he said she was a *very close friend*. She'd met him through Don's ex-wife, Amy. Amy was a dental hygienist and Laney the receptionist for a dentist, Frederick Shaw, who just happened to be Laney's husband. Shaw fired Laney as soon as they separated and when Amy went home and told Don what had happened, Don approached Laney and offered to represent her in the divorce. Then, a short time after her divorce was final, Laney asked Don to represent her in the personal injury suit.

I really wanted to talk to Laney about Don and I think it was the fact that I was delivering her brief when I found his body that made me want to talk to her before I spoke with anyone else. That, and the fact that I suspected they might have been closer than Don had acknowledged. Her name, address, and phone number were all in the file. I took everything back to the kitchen and dialed her number, not really expecting to get her at that time of day.

"Hello," said a weak, weary voice.

"Is this Laney Shaw?" I asked.

"Yes," she answered in the same sad tone.

I took a breath. "I was a good friend of Don Balstrum."

I heard a little groan but nothing more.

"I take it you've heard the news," I said in a soothing voice.

"Yes," she said.

"I'm really sorry," I said. "I was working on your personal injury case with him and he told me you were very close friends."

Laney didn't respond so I told her about my business and how I came to be writing the brief. She said she'd already known of my involvement, which made everything a lot less awkward for me. I told her why I was calling and why I wanted to see her.

"Oh," she said. Then she said it again. "I guess that would be all right. When did you want to see me?"

"Whenever it's convenient for you," I said.

"Well...I don't have a job anymore, so you could come today if you want. I'm not doing anything." Her voice still had that forlorn and hopeless tone.

"Today would be fine with me," I said. "What time would be good for you?"

"Any time's okay. It doesn't matter."

"How about if I come at twelve-thirty and I'll bring us some lunch?"

"Sure. I'll see you then."

"What sort of sandwiches do you like?"

"Anything," she said. "It doesn't matter."

I went back to the library and tried to work, but it took me a good half hour to get into it. I couldn't get Laney off my mind. She'd sounded so unhappy I just couldn't stop thinking about it. I considered asking Mike to come with me to see her but I decided against it. I didn't think she'd appreciate the added intrusion, and what I really wanted was a woman-to-woman talk if I could get her to talk at all.

At eleven-thirty, I put away my work, said goodbye to all, and drove to the nearest grocery store. I bought two kaiser rolls, deli turkey, coleslaw, and some juice. I added a bag of oatmeal raisin cookies, paid for the groceries, and headed for the south side of Milwaukee.

Laney lived on Twenty-fourth Street just off of Oklahoma, right near the bus route I'd taken every-day to my high school (St. Mary's Academy, which is no longer in operation, I'm sorry to say), and very close to the South Side Garden Center where they sell those old-fashioned flocked Christmas trees in just about any color you want. Laney's house was made of a tan-and-cream mottled brick with a dark brown roof and brown shutters. She had a small front yard and barely any side yard. I rang the bell and she answered in less than ten seconds, though more than half of that time was used to release a trio of deadbolts.

I smiled at her and she smiled back with large, bright brown eyes and lips painted a rosy pink. Her hair was a soft, fine, honey blond, cut just above her chin, and her skin was smooth and lightly tanned. She was wearing a pale pink cotton sweater and faded denim jeans.

I said, "Hi, I'm Beth Hartley," and offered her my free hand.

"I'm Laney," she said. "Why don't you come into the kitchen? It was so nice of you to bring lunch. You didn't have to do that."

"It wasn't any trouble," I said. "It's the least I can do for taking your time."

She stopped and looked at me for a moment. "It's not a bother," she said. She looked as if she were about to add something but she turned around in-stead and resumed walking.

Her living room had an "educated" look to it: floor-to-ceiling bookcases on each side of a gold leather couch, a telescope and a good deal of camera equipment near the front window, an upright Steinway piano, a stereo and CD player but no TV, and fine-art prints on pure white walls.

The kitchen was a little more homey. It had caramel-colored tiles to a chair-rail height and cream-colored semigloss above that. She had a large bay window showing a tiny backyard with a steel fence. The curtains were café style, made of a tiny flower-printed cotton in the same shade as her tiles. The table was maple with captains' chairs and seat covers to match the curtains.

Laney offered me a seat at the table. I took it and started to remove what I'd bought.

"I hope you like turkey," I said. "I have rolls and coleslaw, juice, and some cookies for dessert."

She grinned. "That sounds wonderful. To tell you the truth, I'm starving."

"Good," I said. "So am I."

Laney took some plates and glasses from her cupboard and silverware from a drawer. She had napkins on the table and put one next to each of our plates. She clearly was in a better mood than when I'd first talked to her and I didn't want to spoil it, so I decided to ease my way into the conversation.

I commented on her house and the neighborhood while we ate, talked about my house and my business, and her job. She had trouble believing I was a lawyer. She said I didn't look like one. Well, she didn't look all that much like a retired dental receptionist, either, but I kept *my* opinion to myself. And I'll tell you something else. I may not look much like a lawyer, but I do look *exactly* like an amateur sleuth.

After we'd finished our lunch and cleaned up, Laney made us some coffee to go with the cookies. We were having such a nice time chatting that I was reluctant to bring up Don, but I knew I had to.

"I hope you don't mind my asking you about Don," I said. "I knew about your divorce and everything because Don hired me to work on the personal injury brief. He told me how he knew you and for some reason I got the impression you were pretty close, that you were good friends rather than just attorney and client."

Laney nodded without meeting my eyes.

"I'm not asking you to tell me how close you were," I said. "It's really none of my business. What I really want to know is how much you can tell me about Don and his everyday life."

Laney made a sad half-smile and looked straight at me. "It's okay," she said. "I don't mind telling you. We were very close friends. It started when my husband and I separated. I met Don through his wife—she works for my ex-husband—and he was very kind when he heard I was getting divorced. He offered to represent me and he said he'd take care of everything, and he really did. My husband was harassing me and I was scared to death of him but Don was very protective. We did spend a lot of time together after Don and Amy got their separation but it was purely platonic. Really. We enjoyed each other's company and shared a lot of interests but it was nothing more than that. Neither of us was ready for anything more than friendship.''

"I know what you mean," I said. "After my divorce, I didn't even want to look at a man for close to three years and even after that I barely saw anyone at all."

Laney gave me an understanding smile.

"Did you notice any change in Don's behavior lately?" I asked. "Say in the last few months before his death?"

Laney raised her eyebrows. "Well, he was pretty upset for much longer than that. His own divorce was pretty hard on him."

I nodded. "I knew about that. Do you think there was anything else bothering him?"

She shrugged. "Well, he was worried about money a lot but that was mostly because of the divorce, I think."

"What about after the divorce? Was he bitter or angry about the outcome?"

"Oh, yes," Laney said. "He was furious, to tell you the truth. He thought Amy really took him for everything he had."

"Did she really get that much?" I said, not bothering to hide my surprise.

"Not really," Laney said. "He got the house and she didn't get any part of his law business, although he was worried for a long time that she *would* get a part of his business. She supported him while he was in law school, I guess, so her lawyer was really going after it. Don knew him from other cases he worked on and he said the guy hated him with a passion."

My eyebrows shot up. "Really?" I said. "Do you know his name?"

"Amos Alexander, but I don't know where his office is."

"That's all right. I can find that out. Did he ever say anything about anyone else hating him or disliking him? Or even any Don didn't like?"

Laney shifted her position a bit and frowned. "I'm not sure what you mean," she said.

"Well, to be honest, I'm interested in anything that comes to mind, even if it seems insignificant to you."

Laney shrugged. "The first thing that comes to mind is his brother David."

"He had a brother?" I said. "I didn't even know that."

"They didn't get along very well. I never met him but I know he's a lawyer. He does medical cases and personal injury."

"Had Don had any recent contact with him?"

"Yeah, I think so. He sure complained about him enough. I had the feeling there was something going on between them but I think it was mostly jealousy. His brother made a lot more money than he did."

"Can you think of anyone else he might have been having problems with?"

Laney paused for just a moment before she answered and she started playing with the salt and pepper shakers. "Just his wife," she said, "but that was all because of the divorce."

"Did Don's wife or your husband ever find out about your friendship with Don?"

Laney wrinkled her brow. "Well, sure. I think they both knew we were friends. Why?"

"One of them might have resented it, gotten jealous."

"But there was nothing going on. We were just friends."

I shrugged. "They could have misunderstood."

She shook her head. "No, that can't be it. My husband and I were already separated and so were Amy and Don, so even if we were having a romantic kind of relationship, it really shouldn't have upset anyone as far as I can see."

I nodded. "Did Don have any children?" I asked.

"No," Laney said, "and I think it bothered him a lot. He wouldn't even talk about it. I asked him once if he ever wanted children and he actually got up and left. He was like that about a lot of things. He didn't want to talk about anything. He was really hard to deal with sometimes."

I sighed. "I've had friends like that. Overall, I

really liked them but they'd have this one particular quality that really took a lot of tolerance to put up with."

Laney laughed. "Yeah, that was Don all right."

"What was he like otherwise?" I said.

Laney closed her eyes for a moment before she answered. "Well, he was a good listener and I always felt I could confide in him. I trusted him, too, even though he was sort of a compulsive liar." She wrinkled her nose.

I arched my brows and stared at her. "He was a compulsive liar?" I said.

Laney nodded with an expression of disapproval.

"Why do you say that?" I asked.

"Because he gave me several different versions of every story he told me and it was never even anything important. He lied about almost everything. And then I asked him about it one day and he came right out and admitted it."

"What did he say?"

"He said he'd always lied, ever since he was a kid, and it became a habit after a while. His mother used to warn him that if he didn't stop, no one would be able to believe him when he told the truth because they'd never know if he was lying or not. You know, like the little boy who cried wolf."

I nodded. "Did he tell you why he did it?"

"Yeah. He said everyone always liked David so much more than him so he thought he needed to appear to be someone other than who he really was—someone better—for anyone to like *him,* so he made up stories to build himself up. By the time he grew up, he couldn't stop. It became a way of life, I suppose.''

I stared out her kitchen window and let it all sink in. I had a hard time seeing Don in that light. He'd always seemed so pleasant and open. But then, I'd never really gotten to know him. I turned back to Laney.

''You said he didn't like talking about things. Give me another example.''

Laney made one of those mouth-distorting faces and thought for a while. ''Okay, a good example was the service. He was in Vietnam but he just refused to discuss it. Not one word.''

''Well, that's kind of normal, though, don't you think? I don't remember ever meeting a man who was willing to talk about that.''

Laney gave me a sheepish smile. ''Well, I suppose you're right. Neither have I, now that I think of it.''

''What else, if you don't mind my asking?''

''No, it's fine,'' she said. ''It actually feels good to get some of this off my chest. Another big no-no for him was his childhood. If I so much as hinted at it, he'd either change the subject or just get up and walk away.''

''Did you get the impression he had problems with other members of his family besides his brother?''

Laney shook her head. ''I have no idea,'' she said.

"I don't remember him ever mentioning anyone in his family except David."

"How about law school or his practice?"

Laney shifted her position and the salt shaker changed places with the pepper. "He talked about his job a little but it was nothing important."

"Okay. Can you think of anything else that might help?" I asked.

"Not right now," she said, "but if I do, I'll let you know."

"Thanks," I said. "I really appreciate all the time you've given me already. I've learned a lot that I didn't know before I came. I'm glad I spoke to you first."

Laney smiled and I stood to leave. I gave her one of my cards, thanked her again, made a little more small talk at the door, and said good-bye. When I turned around to wave as I reached my car, she had a thoughtful expression on her face. She looked a bit startled when she realized I was watching her, and she waved back.

After I left Laney's, I drove straight to the Milwaukee County Courthouse on Ninth and State Streets. The courthouse is such a magnificent place—marble everywhere, twenty-foot ceilings, carved wood, echoing halls. And it's absolutely mammoth. I felt so privileged the first time I was there—awed, as a matter of fact—thinking about how I'd soon be a lawyer doing truly important business inside those walls. I still felt the same years later, though I never admitted it to anyone.

I got a quick drink at a bubbler (what you non-Milwaukeeans call a drinking fountain, of all things) and went downstairs to take a look at Don's divorce file. Just as Laney had told me, Don had gotten the house and held on to his interest in his law practice. He paid his wife forty thousand dollars for her share of the equity and a good amount of maintenance (formerly known as alimony), but nothing any reasonable person should get overly upset about, particularly someone with Don's income. He'd represented himself, and his wife's lawyer was Amos Alexander with offices on Silver Spring Drive. I wrote down all the pertinent information, got another drink of water, and went on home.

As soon as I got there, I went into the library, got out a new file folder and legal pad, brought it into the kitchen, and started a "Don" file. I've done this for all three of my murder investigations. It makes things so much more organized. I wrote down everything I'd learned from Laney, and about her from Don, and included the impressions I'd made on my own. You never know what can turn out to be important so I try not to leave anything out. I cut out Don's obituary, added it to the file, and then thought for quite a while about what I wanted to do next. I didn't know any of Don's family members but I did know Glen Nolte, his law partner. He'd been in our law school class, too.

I took my file to the library, put it away, and whispered to Mike to come into the kitchen with me. Emily narrowed her eyes but Janice paid no attention. When we reached the kitchen, I said, ''How would you like to come with me tomorrow to interview Glen Nolte—assuming he's in when we get there? I want to take him by surprise.''

Mike looked like a little kid about to go on his first rollercoaster ride. ''Yes!'' he said with a big grin. It was pretty cute, I'll have to admit. I was really excited about having him along, too, though by the next day, I was sorry I'd ever asked him.

TWO

"I WONDER IF HE'S CHANGED since law school," Mike said of Glen Nolte as we walked toward his office building the next morning.

"We can only hope so," I said.

The wind was strong that day and the air damp and cold. A flock of geese passed overhead in perfect V-formation, so high above us they were barely visible. I watched for a while with an awe-inspired smile, straining to hear their distant, beckoning honks. I have always been fascinated by the geese as I watch them migrate, every fall, from the Horicon Marsh to warm, distant lands. Do you know they sometimes reach altitudes of nine thousand feet and can fly as fast as sixty miles per hour? It's truly astounding to think about. And they fly in a V because the air to the side of another goose is less turbulent than the air directly behind. My father taught me those things when I was very young. Every year he took me to see the geese and watch them feed and rest at Horicon Marsh. Over two hundred thousand go through each fall on their way south—one of the many reasons I like fall the best.

I pulled up my collar and picked up my pace. Glen wasn't expecting us (as I had planned) but I knew he was there because I'd called ahead and asked his secretary when he might be available for a conference call that morning. She said he was available all morning until eleven-fifteen, and I said I'd get back to her. Then I told Mike to drop what he was doing—it was time for his detecting debut.

"Hi," I said to the receptionist when we got inside. "I'm Beth Hartley and this is Mike Shepard. We're here to see Mr. Nolte, if he's available. You might tell him that we were in his law school class."

She gave us a bland look, punched a button on her phone, relayed the message, and asked us to sit down. Mr. Nolte would be out in a few minutes, she told us. Mike and I smiled at each other and remained standing. A moment later, Glen came out.

"Beth, Mike, great to see you." He squinted as if he didn't recognize us at all. "Come on back," he added with an abundance of enthusiasm. He put a hand on each of our shoulders and guided us toward his office. Mike sneaked me a quizzical look and I gave him one back. Glen looked the same as the last time I'd seen him, maybe a bit older but still just as pretentious.

You have to understand a few things about Glen Nolte. This guy is the master of posturing. First of all, he insisted all through law school on being referred to as Glen Nolte the Fourth, like we were supposed to be so impressed because his relatives were totally unimaginative when it came to naming their kids. He wore a white dress shirt to school everyday, with French cuffs and solid-gold monogrammed cufflinks. He didn't wear a tie. He wore an ascot. He drove a Porsche, shiny black, and parked it in the no-parking zone right in front of the law school. His license plate read GRN IV. The "R" stands for Redmond. Now tell me this isn't making you sick.

That day, he wore the same sort of shirt and ascot and a suit that looked to be custom made (dark blue with a pale burgundy pinstripe), but he lacked his usual arrogant, condescending manner and his hair was a bit mussed. Glen is tall, about six-two, very slender, with straight ashblond hair and brown eyes. He brought us into his office and very politely offered us seats.

"So," he said when he'd sat down behind his desk (walnut, glass top, modern design). "I assume you're here because of Don."

I drew in a breath and slowly let it out. "Yes," I said. "I wasn't sure you'd have the office open today, but I took a chance."

He winced. "Yes, well," he said, and then hesitated. "I thought of closing up but I've been out of town and the funeral isn't until Saturday. I would've gone crazy just sitting at home thinking about it." He gave me one of those Please-let-me-off-the-hook looks.

"Yeah, I know what you mean," I said, and he smiled.

"Were you out of town when it happened?" I asked him.

"Yes. I had a trial up north." He frowned and looked away.

"How's business?" Mike said, and Glen frowned again.

"Good," he said. "Really great." He shifted in his seat and ran a hand through his hair. "We've been doing quite well, thanks for asking."

"Glen," I said, and paused for a moment. "Do you have any idea at all who might have killed Don?"

"No, I don't," he said. He picked up a paperweight and turned it over to inspect its underside.

"Did he ever anger any of his clients, or more likely the spouses of his clients?" I asked.

Glen looked at me and put down the weight. "Well, there are always hard feelings where a divorce is concerned. But murder? That would be a bit of an overreaction, wouldn't it?"

"Murder always is a bit of an overreaction," I said.

Glen raised an eyebrow but didn't otherwise respond.

I looked over at Mike and he was sitting quietly, passively taking it all in. I looked back at Glen.

"Did Don seem especially bothered by anything lately or was he just his usual self, do you think?"

Glen shifted his position again and looked across the room. "He seemed normal enough," he said.

"Was he spending less time in the office than usual?"

Glen was silent for several moments. "Beth," he

said with a look of annoyance. "Why on earth are you asking me all these questions?"

I glanced at Mike, still mute and immobile, and gave him a dirty look. "Mike and I are helping investigate Don's murder," I said, my eyes still on Mike.

"You're what?" Glen said.

I repeated myself.

"Whatever for?"

"Well, it's become sort of a hobby," I said. "What I mean is, I've done it twice before and I solved both murders and Don was a friend and now he's been murdered so I figured I'd try to do it again and Mike said he wanted to help this time." I took a breath.

Glen gave me a weird sort of look, something between dumbstruck (which he was) and perplexed. Mike didn't move a muscle or say a word.

"I take it you haven't heard about the other murders I solved."

Glen shook his head. "No, I hadn't."

"Well," I said. "Would you be willing to help us?"

Glen's eyes opened wide. "Uh…well, I'm awfully busy," he said. "And I have three kids at home. I hope you'll understand if…"

I looked skyward. "Glen, I didn't mean help us stalk the murderer. I just meant help by talking to us about Don. Just tell us what you know about what was going on in his life."

Glen's shoulders relaxed. "Oh," he said, shaking

his head. "Of course. What would you like to know?"

"Well, to start with, I did get the names of his next of kin from the obituary but I'd like their addresses and phone numbers. If you happen to know at least one of them it would be a big help. And I'd also like to know who some of his friends were."

"I can do that for you," he said. "I know where his brother works and I think I have his home number, as well. I can call him and probably get all the information you need."

"Thanks," I said with a smile. Then I thought for a moment. "Do you know of anything that was bothering him, any problems he was having?"

Glen hesitated just a bit before he answered. "No," he said. "I don't."

I glanced at Mike, who appeared to be dozing off, and slapped him on the shoulder with the back of my hand. "What?" he said in a testy voice as he looked from Glen to me. I rolled my eyes. "Dr. Watson," I said to Glen as I pointed a thumb at Mike.

"What about his divorce?" I asked then.

Glen turned down the left side of his mouth. "He did go off the deep end on that but I can't believe it has anything to do with his death. They may have had a rocky relationship but I can't believe his wife would've killed him. And he wasn't experiencing any difficulties with anyone else that I'm aware of. I'm sorry I can't help you."

"Well, thanks for talking to us," I said as I stood

to leave. I was about to say something else when Mike snored and it made me jump.

"I'll get you the information you asked for," Glen said with an amused grin. "I'll give you a call as soon as I have it."

"Thanks," I said with an appreciative smile. "By the way, what happens to Don's share of the law business now that he's gone?"

Glen gave me a barely subdued sneer. "I pay his estate and the shares are mine. It's all in the shareholders' agreement. If I had died first, it would have been the other way around. You can take a look at the agreement if you don't believe me."

"It's not that I don't believe you," I said, "but would like to see it if you don't mind."

Glen got up without a word, opened the top drawer of one of three matching walnut file cabinets, and withdrew a document. He sat down again and handed it to me. "Paragraph fourteen," he said.

Sure enough, there it was. The document was dated the year they'd started the firm and the agreement was just as Glen had described it. I quickly perused the rest of the document and handed it back. "Thanks," I said.

"Satisfied?" Glen asked.

I nodded.

"So you must agree that my acquisition of his interest could not have been a motive for murder."

I raised an eyebrow. "And why is that?"

Glen shook his head and blew out a breath. "Be

cause if I was going to kill him for the law practice I wouldn't have waited all these years. I could have done it anytime.''

"Oh, I see," I said, in feigned acceptance of his explanation.

We talked a few minutes longer but I wasn't learning anything useful so I decided it was time to go. I gave Glen one of my cards, lifted Mike up by an arm, and said good-bye.

"WHAT KIND OF an investigator are you, anyway?" I said to Mike when we reached my car. "You didn't say a word the whole time and then you fell asleep. I thought you wanted to help."

Mike yawned. "Sorry," he said. "I had a rough night."

I gave him a look. "Andrea again, right?"

He sighed. "Yeah, Andrea. I don't know, she's getting weird on me and I don't know what to do about it."

"What do you mean, she's getting weird on you?" I said after we got inside the car.

Mike zipped his Milwaukee Brewers jacket over his paunch and shoved his hands in his pockets. "Oh, you know. It's the same thing over and over again. Why don't I tell her I love her? Why don't I want to commit? Why don't I ever call her? I see the woman three times a week. How committed can you get? And when am I supposed to call her if I'm always with her?"

"Put your seat belt on, please." He grunted but did it anyway. "Are you hungry? You want to go out to lunch?"

"Yeah, sure," he said. "Let's get a pizza."

"For lunch?" I said.

"Oh, please, oh, please, oh, please."

I rolled my eyes. "Okay, but it has to be Balistreri's." I headed for Sixty-fifth and Bluemound, Balistreri's second location and the one closest to where we were. "How long have you been going out with Andrea?" I asked after I'd driven a few blocks.

"Two years, two and a half, something like that."

"Do you love her?"

Mike groaned and gave me a tormented look. "I don't know," he said in a whiny voice. "Why do you have to ask me that? Why do women always have to analyze and talk everything to death? Why can't you just relax and let things happen?"

I tried not to laugh but I couldn't help it. "Because if we left it up to you guys," I said, "nothing would ever happen, that's why. And why do you have such a problem talking about this stuff? What's the big deal about telling someone you love them? What are you so afraid of? What do you think's going to happen if you say it? Tell me that."

"I did tell her I love her," he said. Nonresponsive but on topic, at least.

"Let me guess," I said. "You told her once and you never said it again."

He sighed audibly. "I told her *twice* and I never

told her I'd changed my mind, so why should I have to say it again?"

"Because she needs to hear it again."

"Why?"

"For reassurance," I said. "Because when *we* love someone we want to tell them every chance we get, so we figure if you're not saying it, it's because you don't feel it anymore."

"That is absolute nonsense."

"Oh, brother," I said. "And why don't you call her?"

"Call her when? When am I supposed to call her?"

"On the days you don't see her. Don't you ever feel like talking to her?"

"I do talk to her. I talk to her when I see her."

"Don't you miss her when you're not with her?"

"Gee. I don't know, it depends on what you mean by missing."

I laughed again. "Oh, yeah, I almost forgot. Men and women use different dictionaries."

He gave me a look of total confusion.

"It means, do you think about her when you're not with her and do you wish you were with her when you're not."

Mike frowned. "Sure, sometimes."

"Okay, so you miss her."

He rolled his eyes, shrugged down into his jacket like a turtle, and looked out the side window. Man-speak for *end of discussion* (I know that because it's in their dictionary).

"WHERE THE HECK were you?" Emily asked me when Mike and I came back from lunch.

"Balistreri's," I said. "Mike had a pizza attack."

"Hmm," she said, and Mike gave her a strained smile.

"Did you learn anything from Don Balstrum's partner?" Janice asked.

"Not much," I said. "But he's going to get me the addresses and phone numbers of Don's family and friends. Oh, and he gets Don's share of the law practice."

Emily frowned. "Well, he just buys him out right?"

"Yeah," I said.

"So, big deal. It's done that way all the time."

I gave her a look that said Well-of-course-I-know that, but I still had my suspicions. It was almost two and I hadn't done a thing all day (business-wise, that is) so I figured, what the heck, why start now? I went to the kitchen and gave Amy Balstrum's lawyer, Amos Alexander, a call. He was in but unavailable. I left a message that I needed to talk with him about Don Balstrum's death and that it was very important. I made a note in my Don file regarding the date and time I'd made the call, and summarized what I'd learned from Glen. Then I called Brian but he wasn't there.

I made myself a cup of tea and was busily making plans about how to approach the investigation when

Glen called. He had the list ready for me and said I could stop by anytime before six to pick it up.

"How about now?" I asked.

"Okay by me," he said.

"AS YOU ALREADY KNOW from the obituary, his brother's name is David, he has a sister named Ann Avery, and both his parents are still alive," Glen said as he handed me a sheet of paper. "And there's his ex-wife, of course. Their addresses and phone numbers are all here. The only friend I know about is a fellow named Abe Parsons but I don't know where he lives and David didn't know either but his folks might, so you can ask them when you talk to them. He and Don were childhood friends."

"Thanks, Glen," I said. "This is a big help. I really appreciate it."

"No problem," he said. "Have any leads yet?"

"No," I said with a laugh. "I haven't even talked to anyone except for you and Laney Shaw, the client I was doing the brief for."

Glen frowned. "The brief?" he said.

"He was doing a personal injury case for one of his divorce clients and he hired me to write a summary judgment brief."

Glen adopted a thoroughly perplexed expression and then looked away.

"You didn't know?" I said.

He started a bit. "I'm sorry, what did you say?"

"You didn't know he'd hired me to do a brief?"

"No," Glen said. "No, I didn't."

WHEN I GOT BACK, I had a message from Amos Alexander. He said to call that day before five or in the morning before ten. I called him right back, introduced myself, told him of my relationship with Don and what I was doing, and asked if I might speak to him personally, sometime in the near future. At his convenience, I added after his long pause.

"Of course," he said. His voice was kind. He sounded old, I guessed seventies or even eighties, but I didn't think it was likely he'd been practicing that long. "I have a full calendar tomorrow except for forty-five minutes between twelve and twelve-forty-five. If you don't mind talking while I eat my pastrami on rye, you're welcome to stop by."

"That would be wonderful, Mr. Alexander," I said. "Thank you very much."

A few minutes later, Brian called. "Can I stop by in a little while?" he asked. His voice was pleasant, but not sociable, if you know what I mean.

"Sure," I said.

"I'll see you in twenty minutes." He hung up without saying good-bye. Not a good sign.

"THERE WAS A MESSAGE from you on Don Balstrum's voice mail," Brian said with a tight jaw when I gave him a hug. He didn't hug me back.

"So?" I said.

He left his coat on and started to pace. "Beth," he

said. "You're on tape saying you'll be at Don Balstrum's office to deliver a brief almost precisely at the time of his death."

"So?" I said again. "You knew I was there. You saw me. And I already told you I left him a message. What could you possibly have to be upset about?"

He paced around the room, came over to me, took hold of my arms, and kissed me. Then he held my face in his hands, kissed me again, turned around, and left. Believe it or not, that is just about the closest I ever get to communication with that man. The trouble is, I really, really like him. He's generally very kind, and not just to me but to everyone. He seems to value things that matter and not get hung up on things that don't. He's easygoing and rarely angered, *except* when it comes to my murder investigating. That is something he just can't seem to handle and it brings out a side of him I truly don't like. I'm not sure he likes it either but it doesn't seem to matter. Every time I get involved in one of these things, the wonderful, gentle Brian I know and love just disappears and That Homicide Detective comes out. His good qualities so far outweigh the ones I don't particularly like, though, and I can't stand to even think of losing him. On the other hand, I don't see why I should have to give this up just because he wants me to. Why can't he just get over whatever's bugging him?

As soon as I calmed down, I called David Balstrum at his office and was told that he was spending the day at home. I called him there and asked if I might meet with him sometime to talk about Don. He invited me to stop by his house at two the following day. My calendar would be looking like Mr. Alexander's pretty soon.

THE NEXT DAY was Friday, October 16. Mrs. Gunther came in early with snowflakes melting on her hat and sat down with me at the kitchen table. This was unusual behavior on her part. I decided something must be wrong. After a long inquisition about the murder, my family, and how things were going with Brian, she let out a loud sigh and stared unhappily out the window.

"Is everything all right?" I asked.

She sighed again but didn't answer.

I made a guess. "How's Erma?" I said. Erma is Mrs. Gunther's sister and she'd been in very poor health for many, many years.

Mrs. Gunther shook her head, then looked straight at me with tears in her eyes. "Oh, Beth," she said. "They think she may have cancer." Then she started to cry.

"Oh, my gosh," I said. I moved my chair closer to hers and put my arms around her. "Maybe it's just a false alarm. They don't know for sure?"

She shook her head.

"How is she feeling? Is she in pain?"

Mrs. Gunther's face folded up into what looked like a prune and more tears came out. "Yes," she said as she nodded. "It's her stomach. That's why I took her. She called Wednesday night and asked me to take her to a hospital. She couldn't call 911, she said. She doesn't trust them to answer the phone.''

I smiled to myself and put a hand on Mrs. Gunther's shoulder. Then I got up and made her some tea and toast (her favorite snack). She drank the tea but didn't touch the toast. After we talked a while longer, I sent her home for the day. She didn't argue with me when I suggested it so I guess it was the right thing to do.

I forced myself to work until eleven-thirty, had a chicken sandwich for lunch, and headed for Mr. Alexander's office on Silver Spring Drive. The traffic on I-43 was pretty heavy so it took me a bit longer than I'd anticipated but the office was easy to find. It was in a big, relatively new building, visible as soon as I exited the expressway. I parked in the lot, told the receptionist I had an appointment from twelve to twelve-forty-five, and asked if Mr. Alexander was in.

She looked at her watch, pursed her lips, and raised her chin. ''It's not quite eleven-fifty-five,'' she said. ''Please take a seat.''

I tried to smile but I'm not sure what it really looked like. I sat down, picked up a magazine, and paged through it. I kept checking my watch and so did she. At precisely twelve o'clock, she picked up her phone and spoke so quietly I couldn't hear her.

''Mr. Alexander will see you now,'' she said when she hung up.

I stood up and started to walk back but she held

up a hand, palm forward. "Please," she said. "Mr. Alexander will be out to show you in."

In less than a minute, an elderly man at least eighty years old walked toward me at a brisk pace with a welcoming grin and extended hand. I took his hand and smiled back. "Amos Alexander," he said in a friendly voice.

"Hi, I'm Beth Hartley," I said.

"Well, come on back to my office, Ms. Hartley." He put his right hand lightly on my shoulder and guided me in the direction of his office. He was a large man, over six feet, with big, wide hands and feet. His complexion was a ruddy pink, crinkly around the eyes from years of smiling. His hair was gray, his eyes a deep blue, and his midsection rather excessive. He looked a little like Santa Claus in a wrinkled dark blue suit and well-worn wing-tip shoes.

His office was conservatively decorated, neat and orderly. The desk was walnut, very plain; his chair, black leather; and the wing chairs in front, a beige, red, and blue stripe. The curtains were beige and the credenza and bookcase matched his desk. He sat down in the leather chair and offered me one of the others.

A moment later, a woman in her mid-forties with orange-blond hair, a fake-looking tan, and big fashion rings on everyone of her fingers walked in after a short knock and handed him a brown paper bag and a Styrofoam cup.

"Thank you, Mrs. Stone," he said.

"You're welcome, sir," she answered back.

He looked at me with an apologetic smile. "My lunch," he said. "Do you mind?"

"Not at all," I said. "I don't want to interrupt you anymore than I have to."

He smiled but didn't answer because his mouth was full.

"I know you don't have much time so I'll make this as quick as I can," I said. "The reason I'm here is that I was told by one of Don Balstrum's friends that you and he didn't get along at all and that you were actually very hostile toward each other."

Mr. Alexander raised a brow as he took a sip of whatever was in the cup. Then he frowned and leaned forward. "Ms. Hartley," he said with a serious tone, "Mr. Balstrum and I often opposed each other in court and naturally there was a certain amount of, shall we say, agitation. You're an attorney yourself. I know you understand."

I nodded. "I do understand that but I'd gotten the impression that his friend was talking about something else, something more personal."

Alexander frowned again and took a bite of his sandwich. He chewed very slowly, swallowed, and took another drink. Then he shook his head at me.

"Ms. Hartley, I can assure you there was no personal animosity on my part toward Mr. Balstrum. I certainly can't speak for Mr. Balstrum but I can honestly say that I never detected any such feelings on his part toward me. I don't know what more I can say on the subject. I'm afraid his friend was misled or that he simply misunderstood.''

I sighed. I realized that Alexander may very well have been totally unaware of Don's feelings.

''Was the Balstrum divorce a particularly difficult one?'' I asked.

Alexander took a deep breath and leaned back in his chair. ''So that's it,'' he said. ''Balstrum represented himself, I'm sure you know, which made every stage of the proceedings exceedingly cumbersome. There's no objectivity, you see, no real possibility of reasoning objectively or even sanely, in his case. You know as well as I that it's never a good idea for a lawyer to represent himself.''

I nodded. ''So did you get into any big arguments? Do you think that's where this came from?''

Alexander pursed his lips. ''It may be,'' he said thoughtfully as he nodded several times. ''We had some rather heated exchanges near the end, I'm ashamed to say.'' He gave me a sheepish smile. ''I'm an even-tempered man and I like to believe I've always been as fair as I know how, but we all have our limits. I hope you see my point.''

I smiled. ''I do,'' I said. ''What was it you argued about?''

Alexander hesitated a few moments so I said, ''I'm not asking you to tell me anything that's confidential.''

He took another, rather large bite of his sandwich.

Then a long drink. His lunch was of great use to him in more ways than one.

"The biggest bone of contention was the property distribution and maintenance," he said. "Balstrum fought us tooth and nail every step of the way. I went after everything Mrs. Balstrum was entitled to under the law. That's my job as her attorney. I'd be committing malpractice if I did anything less."

I nodded and looked at him as if I expected him to continue. So he did.

"He may very well have taken it personally," Alexander said. "Clients lose a good deal of objectivity during a divorce and there was no reason why Balstrum would have been any exception. Divorce attorney or not, he was a human being with human frailties like us all, yes?"

"Yes," I said. "So, what you're saying is that you had no reason to..." I paused as I tried to frame my question as fairly as I could.

"That I had no reason to kill him?" he said with an expression combining amusement with consternation (a bit heavier on the consternation).

"Well, that's not exactly what I meant. I don't really..."

He interrupted me. "There's no reason to apologize, Ms. Hartley, and no point in beating about the bush. That's why you're here, isn't it? To form an opinion regarding the possibility of my murdering Mr. Balstrum?"

I felt myself blush. "Partly," I said, sounding guilty.

"Then let me set you straight. I did not kill Mr. Balstrum and I had no reason to do so. Do I strike you as the type of man who would murder someone? Do you really believe I could have done it?"

"Mr. Alexander, no, I don't believe you did it. I'm not positive, of course, but I do not think that you did. As for the way you look, no, you do not look like the type of person who would kill someone, but murderers very often don't. And people who never even contemplated such a thing can be pushed to a point where they just lose it and they do kill someone. People lose control over themselves. Even the most normal, well-adjusted, well-bred people like you and me. I really believe that under the right circumstances it could happen to anyone. I know that's a scary thought but I'm thoroughly convinced of it."

A frown swept over Alexander's face and he remained quiet for several moments. "There's a lot of truth in what you say," he said at last. "Of course. You're quite right." He sighed and looked at me. I wasn't sure if he meant to continue so I waited a few moments and when he still hadn't said anything I asked, "Can you think of anything that might help me?"

He turned down the corners of his mouth. "No, young lady, I cannot. I'm truly sorry. I wish I could be of service to you."

I stood up and extended my hand. He took it and

placed his left hand on top of mine. "It was a pleasure meeting you, Ms. Hartley, and I wish you the best of luck. Mr. Balstrum's family is fortunate to have someone who cares so much."

I smiled but it was a sad one. "You've been helpful," I said in a sincere voice. "Thank you."

It was twelve-forty when I left Alexander's office and I wasn't due to see David Balstrum until two so I stopped for some coffee and made a few notes about the case while I passed the time. At one-fifteen, I drove to Fox Point on the far north side to meet David. Laney had told me that he had always made more money than Don but the extent of his wealth still took me by surprise. David lived in a mansion by anyone's definition. It overlooked Lake Michigan and the grounds were as extensive as the terrain allowed. There were seven bathrooms, five fireplaces, maid's quarters (no longer used as such), a kitchen as big as one you might see in an old English country manor, a library, a morning room, a conservatory, and an elevator (it didn't work). I saw it all with my own eyes. David gave me a full tour.

But that was after we'd talked and I'd received quite a shock.

THREE

WHEN I ARRIVED at David's house, I was asked by a woman dressed all in white to wait in the "morning room," which was off to the right of a three-storied, cathedral-ceilinged foyer. The room was light and airy, painted a subtle, soft aqua and decorated in taupe, ivory, and the palest of greens. The furniture was highly polished mahogany, Duncan Phyfe, I think. An enormous silver vase of white roses was displayed on the mantel of an ivory marble fireplace. It was afternoon, of course, and the room was in shadow but it had a serene and quiet quality even without the morning sun.

A few minutes after I sat down, the woman who'd shown me in returned, said David would be a few minutes, and asked if I'd like coffee. I said yes and she was back within five minutes with a tray holding one cup of coffee, cream and sugar, and a white linen napkin. The cup was bone china, the kind with the handles you can't get your fingers into.

I had just gotten what I thought was a reasonably good hold on the cup when he walked in. I stood up and gasped, letting the cup fall to the carpet.

"*Don?*" I said in a squeaky voice.

He looked at my spilled coffee with a mixture of

annoyance and amusement, walked out, and returned a few moments later with the same woman. She began to clean up the mess without a word.

He held out his hand to me with a snide smile and said, "David Balstrum. Glad to meet you."

I opened my mouth but nothing came out.

"I take it no one warned you," he said after he led me to the library where he waved me to a tan leather chair and took a seat behind the desk (oak stained very dark, lots of carving).

I shook my head.

He let out a nasty little laugh. "Kind of scary, isn't it?"

I tried to smile. "You were identical twins?" I managed to say.

He opened a palm and shrugged. The answer was obvious.

"I'm sorry about the coffee," I said a few moments later. "I was just so shocked when I saw you. You look exactly the same. Well...obviously."

His expression softened a bit. "I should have made sure you knew before I popped in on you like that, but to be frank I just assumed Don would have told you."

"He never even mentioned you," I said, and immediately regretted it, but David didn't seem to be bothered by the revelation.

I didn't like him much. He leaned back in his chair and gave me a sort of half-grin that really annoyed me. Though he looked exactly like Don and even shared a lot of his mannerisms, his demeanor was different. There was a rudeness or harshness I'd never seen in Don.

"So, you went to law school with Don. Tell me, what was he like as a student?" David said.

A strange question, I thought. "He was pretty quiet," I said. "I never really formed an impression of him as a student. I think he did pretty well, though, didn't he?"

David shrugged.

"What do you do?" I asked.

"Plaintiffs' medical malpractice and personal injury."

"So you're a lawyer, too."

He nodded.

"Why didn't you go to law school with Don?"

"I went to the University of Wisconsin eight years before Don started at Marquette. I guess the bug just bit him later than it bit me."

I smiled, a little. "Where'd you go to high school?" I said. I didn't really care where he'd gone to high school but I was still so flustered that I was having trouble coming up with anything sensible to say.

"Fox Point," he answered with an amused grin.

"I take it from your expression you enjoyed it?"

He laughed. "Yeah, we had ourselves some rollicking good times."

"So you and Don got along pretty well, then, huh?"

His hesitation was barely noticeable. "Yeah, sure," he said.

"Did you see him much?"

David opened a palm. "As much as we needed to. We were both busy with our practices, though. You know how it is."

"When was the last time you saw him?"

"Two, maybe three weeks ago."

"And how about before that?"

Now he was starting to look annoyed. "I really don't recall. Does it matter?"

"No, not really," I said. "I'm just trying to get an idea how much contact you had with him because I was wondering if you were in a position to notice any recent changes in his behavior."

David relaxed his shoulders. "I see," he said. "To be frank, I believe there was something bothering him. He seemed on edge the last several times I saw him."

"Do you have any idea what it was?"

"Well, his divorce, for a start. That wife of his was nothing but a leech. She did everything she could to bleed him dry."

I gave him a rather skeptical look without actually meaning to. He sort of sneered back. "There was something else, too. I had the distinct impression he was having some sort of difficulty with his law partner but he wouldn't discuss it with me."

"Then how did you form that impression?"

"Vague references, things he said from time to

time. I can't recall anything specific but I noticed an edge to his voice whenever he spoke of him and there was an obvious tension between them whenever I saw them together.'' David sat back in his chair and watched my face.

"When did all that start?'' I asked.

He stroked his chin and thought for a while. "Maybe eight to ten months before his death,'' he said. His tone was matter-of-fact, nonchalant. Kind of weird.

"Did he ever discuss his financial affairs with you?''

"Of course not,'' David answered with an abruptness that startled me. "But I'm sure he was in very sound shape. His practice was extraordinarily successful and he didn't have any significant debts or expenses.'' His face clouded over and he narrowed his eyes. "Except for the maintenance payments to his miserable ex-wife.''

"He never had any children, did he?'' I said, hoping I'd moved onto a safer topic.

"No,'' David said, and his face was creased with tension. I changed the subject again.

"How about you?'' I said. "Are you married?''

That got him to smile but it sort of crept up on him. "Yes,'' he said in a more relaxed tone. "My wife's name is Cassandra.''

"Do you have any children?''

"Two boys,'' he said. "I haven't seen them in

years. Feels like I barely know them,'' he added with an odd laugh.

I really didn't know what to make of him. His personality was disturbing to me and I couldn't even begin to gauge how he'd react to any one of my questions. It was making me very nervous.

"How long was Don married?" I said, forcing myself back to my intended topic.

"Twenty miserable years," he said, again with a vituperative sneer.

"So he was pretty unhappy, huh?"

That time I got several slow nods and a look of loathing that appeared to be directed at me rather than Don's ex-wife. I suddenly acquired an overwhelming desire to go home. I couldn't stand being with him. The differences in character between David and the Don I remembered were startling. Don had so much warmth and compassion, or so it seemed, but David struck me as a cold, callous machine. And a very odd one, at that.

"Well, then I guess it's good they got divorced," I said, determined not to let him intimidate me. "Do you think she'd be willing to talk to me?"

"Ha!" he said as if he'd barked. "*Willing?* She'll probably jump at the chance. You can bet she'll be there tonight, gloating."

"Oh, the wake's tonight, I almost forgot."

David curled his upper lip and glowered at me. I sighed and regarded him for a few moments. I was getting tired of getting nowhere and really tired of him. "Do you have any idea who killed him?" I asked in a weary voice.

From the start of the conversation, his face had been a virtual videotape of his emotions. At that moment, impatience and condescension were battling it out and condescension was winning. "No, I do not," he said in a voice to match his expression.

"Well, I really can't think of anything else to ask you," I said as I hurried to stand up. "If you do think of anything, would you give me a call?"

"Certainly," he said with a half-smile. Then he offered to give me a tour of the house. I was so desperate to escape his company I actually said no but then I changed my mind. I just couldn't help myself.

"Do me a favor," he said when we'd finished the tour. "Keep me abreast of things as you go along."

I said I would and I gave him one of my cards.

It had gotten colder and the sun had disappeared behind a cover of dull gray clouds. There was a brisk wind creating frantic little swirls of dead leaves and dry snow at my feet. The snowfall was light and probably wouldn't accumulate to much of anything, but it was only mid-October and I just wasn't in the mood.

I got in my car, turned on the heat (which doesn't work very well), and sat for a while, feeling down, though I didn't know why. I think I missed Don, which didn't make much sense because I hadn't known him all that well and I'd only seen him once since law school (well, twice, if you count the time he was dead). Maybe it was talking to David, who looked exactly like him, that was bothering me. Or maybe it was just David. He was such a jerk.

It was after three and the wake was at seven (actually, it was a viewing, since Don wasn't Catholic). I made myself a cup of tea when I got home, got out my Don file, and added some notes about my meeting with David. After that, I listed the names of the other people I wanted to talk to. So far I had Ann (Don's sister), his parents, Don's ex-wife, maybe Cassandra, and Abe Parsons, the friend Glen had told me about. If Parsons came to the viewing, I'd save myself the trouble of having to look for him. I was putting the file away when Janice walked in, filled her mug with coffee, and added a little cream from the refrigerator.

"Where's Mrs. Gunther?" she said. "Isn't she supposed to be here today?"

"Yeah," I said with a sigh. "I sent her home. She came in early and she was really upset. Erma might have cancer."

"Oh, no," Janice said, and sat down at the table.

I matched her sad look. "Well, they're not sure yet. She may be all right."

"Boy, I hope so," Janice said, and was silent for a few moments. "How's the investigation going?" she asked then. "What was his brother like?"

I laughed. "Oh, my gosh, you're never going to believe this. His brother David is Don's identical twin but I didn't know it until I saw him."

Both Mike and Emily walked in in time to hear that and they both exclaimed at once. "He had an identical twin?'' Mike said. "I never even knew he had a brother until Glen mentioned it.''

"Yeah, come to think of it, neither did I, until Laney told me. She'd never met him, though, so she may not have known they were twins."

Emily and Mike each helped themselves to coffee and sat down with Janice. I frowned and looked at Mike. "How well did you know Don?"

Mike looked suddenly uncomfortable, which confused me but I didn't comment on it at the time. "Well enough," he said. "He was in Trusts and Estates with me and we used to go over our notes together after class."

"Did you ever talk about personal stuff?"

"Sure, some of the time."

"What did you talk about?"

"You know, the usual. Sports, women." He raised his eyebrows a few times in a modified Groucho Marx imitation and Emily rolled her eyes.

"I mean personal stuff, like his family or friends or what he did in his free time."

Mike laughed. "What free time? We were in law school."

I let out a breath. "Mike, you know what I mean. What did he say?"

He gave it some thought. "He told me once he wanted to do plaintiffs' med mal when we got out."

I creased my forehead. "That's what his brother does. Plaintiffs' medical malpractice and PI work. I wonder why Don ended up in family law."

Emily said, "Maybe he wanted to practice with his brother but his brother wasn't interested."

I stared at her. "Hey, maybe you're right. I'll have to ask him about that."

I turned back to Mike. "Did he ever talk about doing family law?"

"Not that I remember," Mike said.

"What about friends—did he mention any? Or did he ever say anything about being in any kind of trouble with anyone?"

"No and no," Mike said. "I met his wife, though. *Very* nice."

I gave him a lopsided smile. "Are we talking about personality here, or something else?"

His smile was a little coy. "Both," he said.

AFTER EVERYONE went home, I had a carton of yogurt, jumped rope a thousand times, took a shower, and put on one of my funeral dresses. Dark gray. Very dreary. Then I headed for Zwaska Funeral Home on Forty-ninth and Bradley. I saw David as soon as I arrived and his behavior struck me as sort of strange. He was milling about as if he were at a cocktail party. He'd sneak up on a group of people almost as if he were eavesdropping on their conversation, make his presence known, and shake hands all around with a somber look. He wanted to introduce me to his mother and his sister Ann right away but they were sitting in a corner, crying softly. David asked me to wait while he went to them. He sat down, put his arm around his mother, and kissed her on the cheek. She rested her head on his shoulder and Ann took hold of her hand. It wasn't easy to watch. David came back several minutes later and said it might be best to wait.

"They're taking Don's death very hard," he said sadly. "This probably isn't a good time."

I agreed. I asked him then about Abe Parsons. David looked around the room. Then he touched me on the shoulder. "Come with me," he said.

Abe Parsons was in his late forties (like Don and David), with graying dark hair that gave him a distinguished and extraordinarily attractive look. He was kind and friendly and offered to meet with me sometime during the next week. He gave me a card with his office number and asked me to call.

I saw Glen sometime later and was about to approach him when David saw me and steered me away. "I'd like you to meet my mother and sister now," he said. They were standing and receiving guests so David brought me over and introduced me, told them what I was doing, and warned them I'd be in touch. They didn't look particularly pleased but neither was rude about it. Ann said, "It's nice of you to help." Her mother smiled weakly but didn't state any opposition.

A bit later, I saw David stiffen as he looked toward the entrance. I frowned and watched his face. A man about his age came in with a woman, greeted Don's mother and Ann, introduced the woman, and spent several minutes talking. David kept his eyes on them the whole time.

"Who is that?" I finally asked him.

David answered, his eyes still on the man. "Chuck Barker," he said. "The three of us grew up together but he was more Don's friend than mine." He paused. "Until a year ago."

"What happened then?"

David still had his eyes on Chuck Barker who was now at the casket, looking at the body. "Barker's a stockbroker," he said. "He gave Don a tip about a year and a half ago and pressured him into investing a considerable amount of money. Six months later, the company went belly-up and Don lost everything."

I raised my eyebrows and sighed. "And Don actually ended their friendship because of that?"

David turned to me with a hard look. "It was Barker's fault," he said. "Don was hesitant about the investment but Barker pressured him, insisted he had inside information and Don was sure to walk away with a fortune."

"Well, it was nice of him to come, I guess."

David looked at me like I was crazy.

I met Cassandra a little later. She was cool but polite when David introduced us. He leaned close to her and whispered in her ear and she gave him a faintly puzzled smile.

Don's father didn't show up until an hour after I arrived and David never got around to introducing us. In fact, I didn't see David speak to his father, even once. He'd given him an angry sneer when he walked in and I reached the conclusion he was upset with him for coming so late. Not an unreasonable reaction under the circumstances, I had to admit.

An attractive woman who looked to be in her early forties came alone, spoke briefly to Don's parents and to Ann, and nodded to David. She looked about to approach him but the glare he awarded her was so unfriendly that I think it scared her off.

"Who is that?" I asked him.

"Don's ex," he said, and turned away.

She walked toward the casket and knelt before it for a few minutes. When I saw her make the sign of the cross and head for the door, I intercepted her.

"Amy Balstrum?" I said.

She looked at me and quickly looked away. "Yes," she said, and kept walking.

I introduced myself as I walked with her and gave her a brief explanation of my interest. She stopped and gaped at me.

"I'm trying to solve Don's murder," I said, feeling a little embarrassed. "I've done it before," I added when she didn't change her expression.

She shook her head and snorted a laugh. "I didn't kill him," she said, "if that's what you want to know."

"I didn't really think you had killed him," I said with a smile. "I was more interested in talking to you just to get some idea of what was going on in his life before he died. You only just recently got divorced, didn't you?''

"Yes," she said with a sigh. "It was final three months ago but we'd been separated for more than a year before that, so it's not like I saw him very often.''

"Would you mind talking to me anyway?"

She shrugged. "No, I suppose not. You want to do it now?"

That came as a surprise. "Sure," I said. "But could you wait a few minutes? I want to tell David I'm leaving.''

She shrugged again and I went to find David. He gave me the strangest smile when I told him where I was going. Amusement coupled with distaste, I think. I went to see Don before I left, said a few words to him, and offered a prayer. Then I quickly scanned the guest register, found nothing revealing, and met Amy at the front door.

"Have you ever been to Sweet Java?" I asked her.

"No, but I've heard of it," she said.

"Well, it's only five or six blocks from here and they have really good coffee and desserts. You want to go there? It'll be a good place to talk."

"Sure," she said. "I'll follow you."

The Sweet Java Dessert Café is on Forty-third and Bradley near Good Hope Road. It was bustling with customers when we got there but there were still a few tables available. We each ordered a coffee with cream and took a seat near the windows.

"Don and I were married for almost twenty years," Amy said when we sat down. "The divorce was just final the end of June."

"I'm sorry," I said, wishing I had something better to say.

"Well, that's how it goes," she answered with a shrug.

Mike had been right. Amy was very pretty. Her hair was a dark, rich brown, worn below her shoulders in soft waves, and her eyes were pale green.

"When I met Don," she continued, "he was enthusiastic about everything, especially about us. He was so attentive and sweet, always doing things for me. He acted like I was his best friend. We did everything together. It was like heaven, we were so in love." Then she winced and looked away for a time. "But then life just seemed to get in the way, I guess. I never really knew what happened. Things just started to fall apart and one day we took a look at our lives and realized there was nothing left. No friendship, no passion, just nothing but bitterness and anger."

She shook her head. "You know, people think you can go back to the way things were and start all over, but you can't. You can't erase all those years and everything that went wrong between you. And it's not even a question of forgiveness. You can forgive and forget until the day you die but the feelings have still changed and they're what really count. Sometimes things just go too far and then it's too late to undo the damage.''

Amy stopped and looked at me, her face creased with emotion. When I gave her what I meant to be an understanding and sympathetic look, she said, ''I hope I haven't given you the wrong idea. I still harbored a certain amount of resentment toward Don but I didn't kill him. As far as I was concerned, he was as good as dead the day we got divorced.''

I wasn't sure how to interpret that but I let it go. ''How did the divorce go?'' I said. ''Was he cooperative at all?''

The look on her face said *What do you think?* ''He was a divorce lawyer, you know.''

''Well, that's true. So I assume he did give you a hard time.''

''The worst,'' she said. ''He represented himself to start with and he fought with my attorney over every solitary, nitpicky thing. He wanted everything and I mean everything. The house, the cars, all the money, everything. I got so frustrated at one point I was ready to just give in but my lawyer wouldn't hear of it.''

''Did it work out all right in the end?''

''It did in my opinion. I've been a dental hygienist for years so it's not like I can't support myself, and I was awarded a fair amount of maintenance to bring my standard of living closer to what it was when we were married because it would've gone down quite a lot on just my salary. He kept the house, which was fine with me, and I got my share of the equity. I didn't get any of his business, which was all right, too, although I *did* put him through law school, but the thing that really bugged me was our savings. He was always a little secretive but I knew he was making money hand over fist and we'd saved a lot, but when it came time to produce our financial records I found out he'd invested practically everything and lost it all. I don't know what happened and I don't pretend to know anything about the stock market but he had no right to invest all that money without consulting me. It was my money, too, and I should've had something to say about what was being done with it.''

I couldn't argue with that. ''So you mean there wasn't anything left at the time you got divorced?''

''Very little,'' she said. ''He had enough to pay me the equity I had coming and about ten thousand in addition to that, but that was it. Everything else was gone.''

I was dying to know how much there'd been to begin with but I held myself back. ''Didn't he use a stockbroker?'' I asked instead.

''Nope. He did all the investing himself and never asked for any advice, except for the time he suffered the biggest loss. Some guy he knew from his childhood suggested an investment and Don followed his recommendation. But then he lost everything he put into it. The company went bankrupt six months later. As far as I know, Don didn't know the first thing about investing, but then again, he never even told me he was doing it. I suppose there could be a lot of things I didn't know about him.''

I gave her a sympathetic smile. "How well did you know David?" I asked.

Amy shrugged and took a sip of coffee. "Not very," she said.

"Did Don ever talk about him?"

"Oh, sure. He talked about him a lot, especially in the beginning. David was always a very hard worker. Super-ambitious. He went to law school before Don did and he'd had it all planned out right down to the last detail before he even started high school. Just the opposite of Don. Don never had any idea what he wanted to do. He ended up getting an English degree which didn't get him anywhere job-wise, so he worked in a bank for a while and then he tried selling insurance. He didn't even think about going to law school until he saw how well David was doing."

"Do you know if David started his own firm right away or did he work for someone else?"

"He was working for a big PI firm right after he graduated but then he and another guy started their own firm. Then about five years later the other guy left and David hooked up with Clem Bailey. They do extremely well," she said with emphasis. "They're always in the news for getting some huge multimillion-dollar verdict. It's pretty impressive, I'll have to admit."

"And how did Don feel about that?"

Amy snorted a laugh. "He was horribly jealous.

Don was always jealous of David. You'd think they'd have been more alike but they were two very different people. David was the golden boy, the one who excelled, the one who was admired and liked. Don was really in his shadow, so to speak, which may account for some of their differences. I think David was always more of an extrovert and an optimist right from the start, so he got more of the attention from the adults. And they'd comment on it all the time. You know, like oh, David's so much more of a personality and this and that, and they'd say it right in front of Don. It was probably something they all dwelled on more than they might have if they hadn't been twins. It was almost like they were looking for differences, you know what I mean? Like they wanted to find them. Maybe it was just a way to tell them apart, but at any rate, I think it had a really negative effect on Don, growing up, and then it just stuck with him. He always seemed to see himself as inferior to David and I know it bothered him a lot.''

"That's pretty sad when you think about it."

She looked at me for a moment. "Yes, it is. You're absolutely right. But that's all ancient history now. He was out of my life months ago and now he's just out."

"Well, that's for sure. So you don't have any idea who killed him?"

Amy widened her eyes. "What, are you kidding? No way. He certainly got on my nerves a whole heck of a lot but I can't see him getting anyone to the point of wanting to murder him."

I didn't want to let on that Laney had told me about Don's habit of lying, but I couldn't help asking her something about it. "Did you feel you could trust him?" I said.

She frowned at me. "Well, I don't think he ever cheated on me, if that's what you mean."

"How about in other ways? Did you feel like he was an honest person?"

This time her expression was a little guarded and she hesitated just a bit before answering. "Sure," she said. "Why do you ask?"

"No particular reason," I said. "I'm just trying to cover things as they occur to me."

Amy still looked uncomfortable so I let it drop. "Oh, I just thought of something else," I said. "Did Don ever talk about wanting to practice with David?"

That made her grimace. "Yes," she said, "but David wouldn't even give him the time of day when he asked him about it. I'll never forget that. It was the day after graduation. He was so excited, I don't think it ever occurred to him that David would turn him down." She shook her head. "He never forgave him for that and neither did I. I don't think I'd ever seen Don so hurt. And the worst part was he'd asked his father when he was still in law school if he'd hire him as his attorney and he turned him down, too. It was months before I could even get him out of bed in the morning."

"That must have been really hard on both of you," I said.

Amy nodded and looked away with such a pained expression that I decided I'd better change the subject. I'd run out of questions anyway so we just chatted about her job for a few minutes before we left. "Thanks for talking to me, Amy," I said as she walked toward her car.

"You're welcome," she said. "Let me know if you need anything. There was no love lost between us at this point but I still want to help. Whatever he might have deserved, it wasn't this."

"Okay," I said. "I'll keep in touch."

It had rained while we were inside and the air was clean and cool, about forty degrees, rather warm compared to the last several days. I wiped the beads of water from my windshield with my wipers and opened my side window so I could hear the swish of puddles on the road from my tires. I got home at nine-thirty and made some notes in my Don file about my conversation with Amy and the people I'd met at the viewing. I realized as I was writing that I hadn't seen Brian, which was unusual. He always shows up at the wakes and funerals, though he's never caught a murderer that way. I almost called him but decided not to. The funeral was at eight the next morning and I figured I'd see him there.

SATURDAY, OCTOBER 17. I got up at six, showered, and put on a black dress. I had a breakfast of raspberry yogurt and toast, brought a large mug of tea along with me, and drove to the Trinity Lutheran Church on North Twenty-fifth Street. This is a pretty unusual church, by the way. It's actually heated by solar energy collected through the bell tower. Let me tell you, it takes a lot of guts to build something in Milwaukee, Wisconsin, requiring solar energy. Then again, maybe it just takes a whole lot of prayer.

Brian was there, as I'd assumed. He sat next to me, several rows behind Don's family, and squeezed my hand. "Hi," he whispered. "How are you?" He didn't look angry at all.

"Fine," I whispered back, and gave him a warm smile.

"What are you doing after this?"

I shrugged. "Nothing special. I have to go shopping for my dinner with Mrs. Robinson but that's all I have planned."

"Can I go with you?" he said with a plaintive look.

"To Mrs. Robinson's?" I said.

"No, to the grocery store."

"Well, sure. You want to come over for lunch?"

Brian looked at me for a moment. "How about this? I'll take you out to lunch and then we'll go shopping." He gave me such a cute smile I couldn't resist.

"Okay, that would be nice. We haven't done that in a long time."

He turned down the corners of his mouth. "No, we

haven't," he said. "It's been a while since we've done a lot of things."

I looked into his eyes but didn't say a word.

"I really want to talk to you," he said. "Seriously."

I waited for more but that was all he said. "Okay," I answered with an encouraging smile. "I'd like that."

The service was about to begin so we quieted down and Brian started studying the guests—carefully watching, spending time on each one, but never craning his neck or being obvious in anyway. A real waste of time if you ask me, but I love watching him work.

After the service we lingered for a while so Brian could "make a few inquiries," as he puts it, and then went to lunch. We decided on Ma Fisher's on Farwell, next to the Oriental Theatre, because they serve breakfast twenty-four hours a day and we both were in the mood for breakfast.

"Why weren't you at the viewing yesterday?" I asked him after we'd been shown to a booth in the back.

He looked away, scanning the room. "I was there for a few minutes," he said. He didn't look back at me.

I gaped at him in disbelief. "Why didn't you come and talk to me?"

He shrugged, still avoiding my eyes. "I don't know," he said in a low voice. "That's what I want to talk to you about."

I sighed and waited. He finally looked at me with a touch of pink in his cheeks. "Not here, though," he said.

As you might have guessed, the meal was a bit awkward, neither of us knowing what to talk about since we had the upcoming conversation looming over our heads. I ordered an omelette and whole-wheat toast with coffee, and so did Brian. I ate mine but Brian barely touched his.

"Do you want to go buy your food for Mrs. Robinson first?" he said when we got outside. He looked like he'd cry if I said no.

"Sure," I said and wrinkled my brow.

Mrs. Robinson, in case you don't know, is a very sweet old woman of eighty-seven whom I met on the Dave Grezinski case (my first murder investigation). We have a standing date for dinner at her apartment every Sunday evening. I cook most of it ahead of time and heat it up in her oven. That time I was making beef noodle soup with carrots and potatoes and Italian beef sandwiches with gravy. Apple pie for dessert.

We went to Sendik's grocery store on Oakland, got everything I needed and a few things I didn't. Then we went back to my place. While I put the groceries away, Brian sat at the kitchen table and fidgeted. I was watching him out of the corner of my eye. "Would you like some coffee?" I said.

"Sure," he answered, without looking at me. I started a pot, heated a mug of water in the microwave for my tea, puttered around until the coffee was made, and sat down. I handed him his cup and stared at him. A few moments later he looked at me and frowned. "What?" he said.

"Brian, what's bothering you? Talk to me."

FOUR

BRIAN SIGHED and looked away, took a couple of sips of coffee, and sighed again. I kept quiet and waited.

"I've been doing a lot of thinking lately," he said, and I felt a worried look pass over my face.

"I think I owe you an apology and an explanation."

"For what?" I said. I had a few things in mind but I couldn't be sure we were on the same wavelength. We seldom are.

"I think I've been a little unfair with you." He paused. "No, I've been very unfair. I've given you nothing but grief since you got involved in this investigating business. I've accused you of interfering, of getting in over your head in something you know nothing about, but when I really thought about it I realized it was nothing but envy on my part." He took off his glasses, rubbed his eyes, and put the glasses back on. "It's just…I'm sorry, I'm having a hard time with this. This is not easy for me to do." He paused again and I waited.

"I was jealous because you solved two murders before I did and what bugged me the most was that you didn't even come close to gloating about it."

I opened my mouth to say something and closed it again.

"Think about it, Beth. This career is my whole life. I have put years into it and I'd reached a point where I was pretty sure of myself. I really believed I was good at what I did. I thought I'd finally accomplished something and then you come along and do it better than I do and for you it's just a hobby. And then you act like it's nothing at all. No big deal. That made me feel even worse, do you realize that?" His face was bright red by then and he was breathing hard.

I gaped at him for a moment and then leaned toward him. "Brian," I said in the most loving voice I could manage. "You are good at what you do. You're great. You solved more cases than anyone in your department in every one of the last four years. You were the youngest person on the force to make detective. And I've always told you how proud I am of you and I meant every word. The fact that I solved a couple of cases doesn't mean anything. Maybe people gave me information they didn't give you. I'm the kind of person people open up to. I've always been that way. People talk to me, they tell me things. That could have a lot to do with it."

Brian shook his head. "It's part of my job to get people to talk. If I'm no good at that then I'm no good at my job."

"Brian, you are good at it. Just because I can get people to talk, too, doesn't mean you're not good at it, it just means we're both good at it. Can't we both be good at something?''

He looked at me and shook his head with a smile that was grateful and sheepish at the same time. ''Yes,'' he said. ''We can. I think that's what I've been trying to say in my usual inept way. There's no reason why I have to compete with you on this. It's a problem I have. I've always been very competitive. I used to consider it an asset but now I'm not so sure. It's okay to a point but I think I let it get out of hand.'' He smiled again. ''And I'm sorry.''

''It's all right,'' I said. ''I forgive you, I really do, and I'm sorry if I made you feel bad. I was actually trying to make you feel better by not gloating. I thought if I downplayed it, it wouldn't threaten you so much.''

Brian laughed and brushed a finger across my cheek. ''Well, I guess I was already feeling threatened so I automatically took it that way. I'll do better, I promise.'' He squeezed my hand. ''I'm going to do my best not to give you a hard time this time around, but *please* try to be careful and call me the minute things start to heat up.''

''I will,'' I said. ''I promise.''

We hugged and kissed for *quite a while* after that and Brian stayed for the rest of the afternoon. We played Monopoly, went out for ice cream, and then went to a movie at the Oriental Theatre. If you haven't been to the Oriental, by the way, you really have to see it. It truly is one of a kind. It's the most elaborately and exotically decorated theater I've ever seen. Buddhas, dragons, griffins, and lions jump out at you from every corner and everything is painted the most vibrant and striking colors. Your senses get a little jump-start as soon as you walk through the door.

After the movie, Brian took me to dinner at the Boulevard Inn, my parents' favorite restaurant. It used to be on Sherman Boulevard across from Washington Park but it burned down several years ago and they moved to the Cudahy Tower. We celebrated every special occasion there (at the Sherman Boulevard location) when I was growing up. First communions, confirmations, graduations, you name it and we were there. It's the ultimate in sophistication and elegance with truly superior food. (I'm thinking of becoming a restaurant critic when I get tired of solving murders. What do you think?) I felt so good when Brian brought me home that night. Things would be better between us now, I was sure.

THE NEXT DAY was Sunday, October 18. I got up late, had a leisurely brunch of French toast and fruit, read for a while, worked on a sweater I was knitting, and did some laundry and a few other totally boring household tasks. Then I baked the pie, put on the soup, roasted the beef, sliced it, and made the gravy. After a shower and a quick cup of tea, I headed for Mrs. Robinson's.

Mrs. Robinson lives in an old Art Deco apartment

building right off of Brady Street on the east side of the city. It's the same building in which Janice Grezinski's brother Dave was killed. I worried quite a lot about Mrs. Robinson during that investigation because I was afraid the murderer might think she'd seen or heard something since she has a practice of leaving her door wide open and she lived only one door down from Dave. But everything turned out just fine in the end and we became the best of friends. Even my mother has taken to her and treats her to lunch at Watt's Tea Room once a month. It's a real thrill for Mrs. Robinson and for my mother as well. Every once in a while I go along, but I usually try to let them have that time to themselves. I think it does them both a lot of good.

When I arrived, Mrs. Robinson's door was open and I could hear her puttering around in the kitchen, though puttering may be too strong a word. Mrs. Robinson moves very slowly and carefully. It takes her a good minute and a half just to get from the kitchen to the door and she's pretty well exhausted after the trip. She can't stand up straight and has to strain to look up at me. She was once five feet three, she tells me. It's hard to believe.

I rapped loudly on the doorjamb, called her name, and made a lot of noise, as I always do, to avoid startling her (she's also hard-of-hearing). She jumped just the same and held her hand to her chest when I walked into the kitchen.

"Oh, my dear," she said in a breathy voice. "You gave me quite a fright. I didn't hear you come in."

I smiled and gave her a kiss and a hug. "I'm sorry," I said. "Hang on, I have one more trip."

I went back down to the car and got the pie, put the soup and the beef (in a pot of juice) on the stove to reheat, and made us each a cup of tea. It's all part of the ritual we go through every Sunday.

"Now tell me, how was your week?" she said after she'd taken her prerequisite two sips. "I want to know everything you've been doing."

"Well, you're not going to believe it," I said.

Mrs. Robinson tilted her head to the left and peeked up at me. "Don't tell me," she said in an excited voice.

I laughed. "You guessed it. I'm investigating another murder."

"Oh, my dear," she said, straining to sit up. "Now tell me all about it."

I know it sounds kind of disgusting, but it's almost like we both get a thrill out of someone getting killed just so I can figure out who did it. It actually worries me at times but I try not to dwell on it. I told her everything I could think of about Don and David.

"My, how very interesting," she said. When I told her about Amy, she frowned and said, "Hmm."

I frowned back. "What are you thinking?" I said.

"Well, I'm not sure," she said. "But it's a bit peculiar."

"What is?"

"His brother doesn't seem to like the ex-wife at all but you say she's terribly nice. Quite friendly, in fact. It's peculiar, that's all. Wouldn't you agree?"

"Well, I think he's just protective of Don. Don apparently resented her for the way she handled the divorce and I think David is just taking Don's side."

"I'd keep an eye on her," Mrs. Robinson said, and it sounded like an order. "And what about this twin business?"

I laughed. "Yeah, that was quite a shock. You know, I've always been intrigued by identical twins. I can't imagine what it would be like to have someone else in the world who looked exactly like you and maybe even walked and talked like you. It must be the weirdest feeling. I'll bet the usual sibling rivalry is even worse for them."

Mrs. Robinson creased her brow. "Well, now, I don't know. I read once that twins form a special bond, stronger than any other, and that they're closer than most siblings. They protect each other."

"Well, David does seem very protective of Don, I can't deny that."

"Tell me more about the young woman, Laney," Mrs. Robinson said. "Did she act properly distraught?"

"I don't know," I answered with a frown. "At first she did, and then she didn't. It was strange."

Mrs. Robinson nodded. "I'd keep an eye on her, too. And don't forget that partner of his. I'm not sure I trust him, either."

Well, that covered just about everyone. I smiled and Mrs. Robinson smiled back. "How is your young man taking this?" she said.

"Oh, gosh. He took it very badly at first, just like he always does, but then he came over and apologized. He said he was really sorry and that he was just jealous because he thought I was doing his job better than he was."

Mrs. Robinson gave me a look with a hint of reproach. "My dear, you know men do need to feel they are successful in their work. That may sound old-fashioned but I believe it's true even today. I do believe they can't help themselves."

I laughed though I tried not to. "Well, I think we all need to feel successful in our work," I said.

She nodded. "Of course, dear. You're perfectly right."

Our dinner was ready by then and we ate at her dining table set under the hanging chandelier in the main room. Mrs. Robinson raved about every little thing, as she always does, and we talked some more about Brian and quite a bit about Mrs. Robinson's late husband. She'd barely mentioned him before that night.

"He was a good, kind man," she said in an affectionate voice. "A simple man, but good, through and through. He never had a harsh word for anyone, always a smile. Didn't let the little things bother him, either, even when we were young. Now there was a man who knew what was what at a very early age. It takes some people a lifetime to learn those things. So many never learn at all.'' She sighed a heavy sigh and looked down at her hands.

"How old was he when he died?'' I asked in a gentle voice.

"Seventy-four,'' she said. "It's been thirteen years since I lost him. He lived a good long life but I do miss him terribly.'' She looked at me for a few moments as if she were considering whether to go on.

"Loneliness is the saddest part of growing old, you know. I don't deny it's harder to do the things we take for granted when we're young, but it's the loneliness that weighs on us. It's hard to be alone and know your time is near. Maybe that makes it easier to accept, though. I do look forward to being with Howard again.''

My eyes filled with tears and I felt a lump in my throat but I gave her a loving smile and did my best to move on to another subject. After another twenty minutes or so on less emotionally charged topics, it was time for me to go. I promised to call her during the week to see how she was doing and said I'd see her next Sunday. She gave me a lingering hug and held on as tightly as she could. "My favorite day of the week,'' she said. I kissed her good-bye and left with tears in my eyes again.

Maybe I should spend more time with her, I thought as I was driving home, *or at least call her more.* I told myself I really didn't have the time for much more than I was already doing and then I felt like I was rationalizing. Then I tried to convince myself I wasn't. It's so hard to know my own mind, sometimes. No wonder no one else can figure me out.

At nine the next morning, I called Abe Parsons, Don's childhood friend. We made an appointment to meet at his office at three on Wednesday afternoon. Then I called Ann Avery, Don's sister. She said I could stop by that afternoon if I wished. We agreed on four o'clock, which she said would give us plenty of time to talk before her husband came home.

Mrs. Gunther came in at nine-thirty (late, for her) and looked awful. She had dark patches under her eyes and her hair was disheveled. I gave her a concerned smile and asked her to sit down at the kitchen table. "Are you all right?" I said.

She lowered herself to a chair with some effort, put her handbag on the table, and took off her coat. "I'm all right," she said. "Erma has her tests this morning. I had to take her in last night."

I sighed. "Would you like some tea?" I said.

She shook her head.

"You don't have to stay, you know. The house looks fine the way it is and Erma's a whole lot more important than cleaning, any day."

She gave me a weak smile and squeezed my hand. "If it's all the same to you, honey, I think I'd rather keep busy. Keep my mind off it. I wouldn't do anybody any good over there anyway. Erma wouldn't know I was there. Soon as she's done they're going to call me. I'll go see her after."

I nodded. "Okay," I said. "Let me know if you need anything."

Janice walked in from the library just then with a plate of cookies in her hand. I gave her a quizzical look. She made an unsuccessful attempt to smile and put the plate in front of Mrs. Gunther. "I made you some of those sugar cookies you like so much," Janice told her in a quiet voice.

Mrs. Gunther looked up and shook her head as she gazed at Janice. "You sweet girl," she said. "You sweet girl."

Janice sat down next to Mrs. Gunther. "How's your sister doing?" she asked. I left them alone and went into the library.

Emily and Mike were there, working away. Mike looked at my face and said, "Everything okay?"

I nodded but didn't speak because I couldn't trust my voice.

"You sure?"

I nodded again. "Mrs. Gunther," I said, and my voice cracked.

Emily looked up and frowned, then went back to her work.

"Erma?" Mike said.

"She's having tests today."

He made a sad and understanding face.

We worked until lunch, ate chicken salad sandwiches and tomatoes, and went back to work. Mrs. Gunther left at three-thirty and I left shortly thereafter to see Ann Avery.

Ann lived in Glendale, a little north and west of Whitefish Bay. I-43 was crowded, as it usually is at that time, but a soft drizzle fell, steady and calm, easing some of the tension I'd been holding inside. Luminous golds and reds glowed against the jet blackness of saturated bark and shafts of white light pierced through a cloud, far off in the distance. I felt a brief respite despite Don and despite Erma. Sometimes I truly believe these tiny cameos of nature are sent to me as gifts. Gifts of hope, or maybe just acceptance. I find a peace and serenity in the beauty of nature that I haven't found anywhere else.

It was four-fifteen when I got to Ann's place and almost completely dark. Her house was all brick, set back a good distance from the road with an attached garage that opened on the side. There were two stories with three dormers on the second, and the front door, trim, and shutters were painted what looked like a pinkish-beige. The neighborhood was heavily wooded with no sidewalks. Everyone had a cluster of trees in their front yard. Ann had three pines and two ashes.

I parked in her driveway and by the time I got out of my car, Ann was waiting for me at the door with a welcoming smile. What a change from her brother, David. She looked older than David and Don by at least ten years, which I guessed put her somewhere in her late fifties. She was a bit heavy, sort of stout rather than plump, but actually quite elegant. Her hair was a silvery gray, professionally done in a short wavy style. She wore a gray wool skirt and black flat-heeled shoes—the same clothing I'd seen her wearing at the wake.

I smiled back as I walked toward her and she let me inside. The foyer was small with a floor of terra-cotta ceramic tile and wallpaper with a cream-colored background and a rose, medium blue, and taupe design that reminded me of a Birds of Paradise print, only this one didn't have any birds. The chandelier was gleaming brass and so were the wall fixtures and umbrella stand. I told her how pretty I thought it was.

"I'm so glad you're here," she said, which surprised me a great deal.

I said, "Thank you. It's really nice to hear that. I so often feel like I'm just bothering people."

Ann gave me another kind smile and shook her head. "You're trying to help my brother in the only way you can. I'm touched and very grateful. I don't quite know how to thank you."

I smiled uncomfortably and fumbled around for an appropriate response. "I haven't really done anything yet," I said. "I have no idea who killed him, at this point."

I got a half-smile that time and a slight nod. We walked through the living room, which was also small but beautifully furnished. Ornate floor-to-ceiling bookcases framed the brown brick fireplace. A desk was against the adjoining wall and the coffee, end, and sofa tables were in the same Chippendale style. Everything was dark cherry. The upholstery on the sofa and matching wing chairs was brocade, a subtle peach-and-light-blue print.

We ended up in the sitting room, as she called it, a room in the back that might have been designed as an extra bedroom. It was decorated with oak end tables, a matching entertainment unit, and two unmatching bookcases. The couch and easy chairs were dark green with green, dark red, and beige striped throw pillows. The lamps on the table had wooden bases and plaid shades in colors coordinating with the pillows. The floor was blond hardwood, partially covered by a dark green braided rug.

Ann asked me to sit down and offered me something to drink, giving me a choice of coffee, tea, or juice. I chose coffee with a little cream. She was back within two minutes with two cups of coffee and a carton of half-and-half. After she'd added a bit of cream to her cup, Ann crossed her legs and said, "Now, what can I do for you?"

"Well, what I'd really like is for you to tell me anything you can about Don that you think might be relevant. Actually, anything at all that you wouldn't mind telling me about him. I don't always know ahead of time what information will turn out to be useful. For instance, what was he like growing up? What kind of a person was he? What did he like to do? That sort of thing."

"What was Don like growing up?" Ann repeated. "Well, he was quiet, and very reserved. Altogether unlike David." She laughed just a little and looked like she was remembering. "He preferred to keep to himself. He could sit alone for hours and just think. He was a real daydreamer, that one. And he loved to draw. He drew the most elaborate pictures. Intricate, complex designs. They were quite beautiful, really."

She took a sudden deep breath and closed her eyes. "Well, not all of them," she added. "Some of his paintings were almost frightening. Really quite disturbing."

"In what way?"

She shook her head and shuddered a bit. "They were almost violent," she said. "So full of anger." She shuddered again.

"Did you spend a lot of time with them when you were kids?" I asked.

"Oh, yes, I surely did. I'm quite a bit older than they, twelve years almost to the day, and I watched after them nearly all the time. My mother hadn't planned on them, you see. I didn't know it then, of course, I only learned it after we'd grown up, but it explained quite a lot. My mother was out most of the time." She put a significant emphasis on the word *out*. "As soon as I turned thirteen," she continued, "my mother handed them over to me." The look on her face was cold and bitter.

"That must have been very hard on you," I said.

The revengeful expression turned into a sardonic smile. "It wasn't always easy, I can tell you that. I had my own interests and I quite naturally wanted to be with my friends. If I wanted to go somewhere I generally had to take the boys along, which never set well with my peers. It caused me a great deal of heartache and isolation. I felt different and odd. No one else had to take their younger siblings along and none of them could understand why I had to. After a while, they began telling me that I was welcome only if I came alone. Eventually, they stopped inviting me altogether.''

I sighed. ''That's not easy to take at any age, but particularly not at thirteen.''

Ann gave me a tenderly grateful look and her eyes were glistening.

''Did your mother work?'' I said. ''Is that why you had to take care of the twins?''

''No, my mother did not work,'' Ann said. ''She socialized.'' She gave the last word the same emphasis she'd given the word ''out'' a little earlier.

I nodded and tried to keep my expression as neutral as possible. ''Did Don ever get in any trouble when he was young?''

''Well, they both engaged in a few pranks now and then,'' she said with a laugh. ''But nothing serious, mind you.''

''Do you know if Don ever made any enemies? Or David either, for that matter?''

Ann frowned and shook her head. ''Not that I'm aware of. They were both rather straitlaced. They never got into trouble with the law or went in with a bad crowd. They never used drugs, I'm sure, and neither of them drank, except for socially, of course.''

"Do you have any idea who could have killed him?"

"No, I don't." She creased her forehead. "Do you have any serious suspects?"

"No, I'm afraid not. I'm really just getting started. I haven't talked to enough people yet."

"With whom have you talked?"

"Well...you and David, Amy, Don's law partner, Amy's lawyer, and one of Don's clients. Her name is Laney Shaw. Do you know her?"

Ann shook her head. "No, should I?"

"She and Don were pretty good friends. They spent a lot of time together."

Ann's eyes opened wider and she hesitated for a moment. "No, he never mentioned her." She frowned. "You wouldn't know when this friendship started, would you?"

"According to Laney, it started right after Don and Amy separated. But it was just a friendship," I added. "They weren't actually dating."

Ann nodded as she stared across the room. Then she looked at me again. "What did you think of Amy?" she asked.

"I liked her. She seemed pretty nice."

Ann nodded. "I liked her, too."

"Can you tell me anything about the marriage?" I said.

"There isn't a lot to tell. Just a case of irreconcilable differences, as far as I could determine."

"Well, at least they didn't have any children. That would've made it a lot harder."

"To be truthful," Ann said, "I'm not so sure. You see, that was the cause of a great deal of tension between them. Don couldn't have children. I'm not sure why. Something to do with an illness. It happened in college, I believe. He was very closemouthed about it. In fact, he became quite incensed the one time I brought it up."

"Then how did you find out about it?"

"It was Amy who told me. She came to me one day and she was quite concerned, I can tell you. You see, she wanted children very badly but Don wouldn't adopt. She was hoping I might convince him. I didn't want to get involved but she was quite insistent." She shook her head. "I've always regretted it. Don was furious and I'm afraid he took it out on Amy."

"How do you mean?"

"Well, nothing physical, mind you, nothing in the way of violence, but he was angry, extremely angry. He felt she'd betrayed a confidence. I can't help feeling he was right, though I couldn't blame her. She was quite beside herself."

"What about his friends?" I said. "I've met Abe Parsons and he's promised to talk with me next week. Do you know him?"

Ann nodded. "A very nice man," she said. "Even as a child, he was polite and charming in a peculiarly genuine way. I liked him very much."

I smiled and said, "Did he have any other friends? Currently, I mean. People he spent time with."

She shook her head. "I really don't know the answer to that. The two of them had playmates in the neighborhood when we were growing up but of course they've moved away and I don't know if Don saw any of them after that. As far as high school or college friends, I couldn't say. You see, I was long gone before they'd reached that age. I was out of college and married by that time so I was no longer involved in their day-to-day lives even when they were teenagers."

"How did they get along with your father, if you don't mind my asking?"

Ann let out a short, bitter laugh. "Now there's a question," she said. "How did they get along with Father?" She paused for a few moments and shook her head again. "I suppose they got along as well as could be expected."

I gave her a questioning look.

"My father..." She stopped, then began again. "My father was extraordinarily strict and nearly impossible to please. No one, and I mean no one, ever measured up to his expectations. To this day, I'm horribly uncomfortable in his presence. I'm always on my guard, afraid I'll do the inexcusable, break some unknown or forgotten rule, displease him in myriad different ways."

Ann shuddered a little and her whole body tensed.

"My father was never satisfied with Don. He treated him very harshly, even more so than the rest of us."

"Why was that?" I asked.

"I don't know," she said. "I never understood. I'm sure I never will."

When I didn't respond she frowned and said, "I hope I haven't wasted your time. I don't know what to tell you that will be of any assistance."

"Oh, you've been a great help," I said with a look of sincerity, "though I do think I've run out of questions. If I think of anything later would you mind if I called again?"

"Not at all," Ann said. She asked if I'd like some more coffee and when I declined, she stood up and walked me to the door. "I enjoyed meeting you, Beth. And I can't emphasize enough how much I appreciate the interest you're taking in Donald's case."

I smiled warmly and said thanks, gave her one of my cards, and promised I'd let her know if I made any significant discoveries.

It was barely five o'clock when I left Ann's. The air was cold and so was the rain. It blew sideways, one way and then another, a fine mist that left me damp and shivering by the time I reached my car. All I could think of was hot tea and the phone calls I wanted to make as soon as I got home.

When I was inside the house, I ran upstairs and changed into loose jeans and a sweatshirt—comfortable, cozy, and dry. Then I ran back down, put a mug of water in the microwave, and got my Don file from the library. As I sipped my tea, I alternately made notes regarding my conversation with Ann and held the cup in both hands to warm myself up.

Then I made a list. I had to call Amy and I had to call David. I decided to try David at the office since it was early enough for him to still be there. I was in luck. He picked up the phone himself.

"Balstrum and Bailey. David Balstrum," he said, sounding like his mind was on a dozen different things.

"David, it's Beth Hartley."

"Beth, what's up? I'm extremely busy but I'll give you a few minutes."

I gave the mouthpiece a dirty look. "I wanted to ask if you knew anything about Don not being able to have children and—"

He cut me off. "You don't know what you're talking about," he barked. "He may not have had any children but he was certainly capable of having them."

I could almost see the spit flying through the air. He was so protective and defensive where Don was concerned, it made me wonder if he was even aware of Don's envy of him and his life.

"So you don't know anything about an illness he had in college?" I asked (not knowing when to quit).

"You've been misinformed," he said in a voice seething with anger, "and I've run out of time. I'll talk to you later, Beth." He hung up.

I dialed Amy's home phone number, knowing

she'd no longer be at work, but her answering machine picked up so I left a message asking her to call.

THE NEXT DAY was Tuesday, October 20. Amy hadn't returned my call but it was still early so I decided to try Chuck Barker first. I found a Charles C. Barker on East Kenwood and a Charles B. on South Fifty-eighth. I was ninety-nine-percent sure that Charles C. was my man. I dialed the number and got the housekeeper.

"Oh, I'm so glad someone's at home," I said in a panic-stricken voice. "This is Mrs. Thompson and I have an appointment with Mr. Barker at nine-thirty this morning but I just found out I have to cancel and I lost my little slip with his office number on it and I'm so sorry but I really need to get in touch with him. You wouldn't happen to know the number, would you?" I took a breath. "Please, it's really very urgent."

"Just a moment, I'll get you the number," she said in a voice obviously meant to calm me down. I heard some rustling and a moment later, I had it.

"Thank you so much," I said, still sounding out of breath.

I hung up and dialed Barker's office. When his secretary asked who I was and what my call was in regard to, I told her I was a good friend of Don Balstrum and that the call was in regard to his murder.

It was only a few moments before he was on the line. "Charles Barker here. How can I help you?"

"Mr. Barker, my name is Beth Hartley," I said. "I'm a friend of the Balstrum family and I'm helping to investigate Don's death. Don's brother David suggested I talk with you, if you're willing, about an investment you made on Don's behalf about eighteen months ago."

There was silence on the other end for nearly half a minute, then a loud sigh. "Come to my office at ten-thirty this morning," he said, and he hung up. I had to call back to get the address.

"How would you like to come along on another interview?" I asked Mike when I sat down at my desk.

"When?" he said.

"Ten-thirty this morning. It's a guy named Charles Barker. He's some kind of stockbroker or financial adviser and Don's brother told me he talked Don into making a big investment about a year and a half ago and Don lost a whole bunch of money because of it."

"So?"

"So I thought it might be worthwhile to talk to him. He was someone Don apparently had some really bad feelings for."

Mike gave me a bewildered look adorned with a good deal of sarcasm. "Let me get this straight," he said. "You think this stockbroker guy might have killed Don because Don was angry with *him?* Is this a self-defense theory, or what?"

I closed my eyes and opened them again. "Nooo" I said. "I just think we might learn something from him since they had a relationship that went bad. Who knows? If Don disliked Barker so much, maybe the feeling was mutual. We certainly have nothing to lose by talking to him.'' I was getting annoyed. Why was I defending myself? Why involve Mike at all? I could do just fine on my own.

Mike sighed and turned down his mouth. ''All right,'' he said. ''I guess you're right. I'll go with you.''

''Good,'' I said, though I was no longer sure I wanted him along.

We worked for another hour and then I told Mike we'd better get going. Barker's office was on Good Hope Road and it'd take us a while to get there.

The sky was gray again that day, not a bit of sun poking through, and the air was cold and damp (yes, again). I turned on the car heater and soon we were as warm as could be, but then I couldn't see out my windshield. For that, I needed my air conditioner. I turned it on and Mike let out a few of his favorite expletives.

''Why don't you just get yourself a decent car?'' he said.

''This is a decent car. It just has a lousy heating system. The rest of the car works perfectly fine. I want to get my money's worth.''

''You're not getting your money's worth by keeping it,'' he said. ''You're just getting punished longer for buying it in the first place.''

I had to hold my breath to keep from replying.

Marriage, nagging spouse, were among the words that flashed through my mind. If there's one thing I absolutely hate, it's being criticized and told what to do. I'll keep that car until the engine falls out if people don't stop telling me to get rid of it. What a relief it was when we arrived at Barker's office.

"MR. BARKER, THIS IS Mike Shepard. He's helping me with the investigation," I said after Barker's secretary showed us to his office.

Barker gave Mike a dirty look and waved his hand in the general direction of the armchairs in front of his desk. We each took a seat and Barker sat back and stared at us with cold, lake-blue eyes. He appeared to be about fifty or so. His hair was gray-blond, his skin a pasty beige, and his clothes custom-made—a blue monogrammed shirt, charcoal gray suit, and dark red tie with a barely visible light blue stripe. I didn't like him and neither did Mike. Mike slumped down in his chair, folded his arms across his chest, and squinted at him.

"Well," I said. "I appreciate your seeing us on such short notice."

Barker didn't respond.

I tried again. "I'm sure you're very busy so I'll try not to take too much of your time. If you could tell me how long and how well you knew Don, it would be a good way to start."

Mike turned and looked at me and then looked at Barker.

Barker relaxed his shoulders a bit and sighed. "I knew Don most of my life," he said in a weary voice. "We grew up together."

I gave him a weak smile. "Were you very close?"

Barker winced for a split-second. "Yes, once," he said. "We went to high school together, went out for the same sports, hung out with the same crowd. We used to double-date for pity's sake." He let out a long deep sigh and averted his eyes. "We lost track of each other after we graduated. I went to college out east and he stayed here. When I came back, we started keeping in touch again. Then I put him on to something I thought was a sure thing and it backfired. I didn't make the investment on his behalf, by the way. He did it himself on my recommendation. But I'd been wrong and he lost every penny. He wouldn't forgive me." Barker looked away again. "I haven't forgiven myself."

I gave him a sympathetic look. He didn't seem like such a bad guy after all. "Everyone makes mistakes," I said, "and the business you're in is so risky by nature that you have to expect it to happen sometime or another, don't you?"

He smiled at me, very warmly, in fact. Mike looked at me again and frowned in a really obnoxious way. I glared at him and looked back at Barker.

"Were you friends with David, too?" I asked.

"No," Barker said. "They weren't much alike, believe it or not. David was too arrogant for my taste."

"Didn't they hang around with each other, though?"

"Not in high school. They were just like anybody else. You don't hang out with your brother when you get to be that age. You hang out with your friends."

"Yeah, I guess that makes sense. Did he have any other friends who you think might be able to help me?"

Barker shook his head and shrugged at the same time. "Don had other friends," he said, "but I can't remember anyone in particular and he didn't have any enemies that I know of. I don't know how I can help you."

"Well, neither do I," I said with a sigh. "Did he talk to you about anything really personal back then, like his plans for the future, his home life, anything like that?"

Barker laughed. "Yes, we talked about those things but it wasn't a hot topic, if you know what I mean."

I smiled. "What did he want to do when he grew up? Did he tell you that?"

Barker wrinkled his brow and thought for a few moments. "As I recall, he had some sort of fantasy about being a doctor." He shrugged. "But he never pursued it. He was like that—more thought than action, if you get my drift."

I smiled again and started to laugh. "Well, I know what that can be like. So, I guess I've wasted a good fifteen minutes of your time and I'm not any better off than I was before."

Then he laughed. "Well, I wouldn't say that," he said. "You've met me, now, haven't you?"

"WELL, WHAT DID you think?" I asked Mike when we were back in the car.

"He's a jerk," Mike said. "And why'd you keep smiling at him like that?"

I scrunched up my face. "Like what?"

"Forget it," Mike said.

When we got home, I decided to give Don's parents a try, though I really wanted to see them separately, preferably his mother first. I was in luck. She was at home and he was not.

"I suppose I could do that," she said in a tentative voice after I'd reminded her of our introduction at the viewing and explained what I wanted.

"I've already talked to Ann and David," I said, hoping that might make her feel less reluctant.

"Well, all right," she said. "I guess you could come to the house. Maybe sometime next week."

"Could you possibly make it this week?" I asked in a plaintive voice.

"Well, all right," she said again. Then she paused for a moment. "Why don't you come on Thursday morning? It will have to be early, though. I have a nine-thirty appointment and I'll need to be on my way by nine-fifteen."

We decided on eight-thirty, which I assumed would allow me plenty of time, and she gave me very detailed directions to her house. She seemed to have lost her hesitancy about talking to me and her voice was much more pleasant.

I made a note on my calendar, went into the library, and made another note in my Don file. Then I asked Mike if he wanted to come along.

"Yep, I think I do," he said. "I have a few questions for old Mom."

I raised my eyebrows and laughed. "Like what?" I said.

"You'll see," he answered.

FIVE

WEDNESDAY, OCTOBER 21. I had an appointment with Abe Parsons at three, a brief to work on, and a phone call to make. Amy Balstrum hadn't called me back so I decided to give her another try.

"Amy?" I said when she picked up the phone. "It's Beth Hartley. I know it's early but I was hoping I'd reach you before you left for work. Can you talk to me for a few minutes?"

"Sure, what's up?" she said, sounding wary and nervous.

"I know this may be a touchy subject, but I wanted to ask you about Don not being able to have children."

"Oh. What about it?" Now she was sounding relieved.

"Well, was it true, first of all?"

"Yeah, it was true."

"Did you know about it before you married him?"

She let out a burst of laughter. "Right, now wouldn't that have been nice? I didn't find out until after he let me go through every single fertility test known to man. He flatly refused to be tested himself, like there was no way it could be him instead of me. Well, then the doctor finally convinces him to do his thing and lo and behold, *he's* the one who can't have children.''

''So Don didn't know about it before you got married, either?''

''Oh, right, tell me about it. He knew. He knew it all along. Of course, he swore up and down that he didn't but I wasn't buying that for a minute.''

''Well, I'm sorry about that, I really am. I know what it's like to want children and not be able to have any.''

When she didn't respond with anything more than a ''Hmm,'' I said, ''Amy, I have one more question for you. Before you and Don separated, did you get the idea that he was in some sort of trouble or that he was having problems at the office, like maybe with Glen Nolte?''

It's times like this that I wish I were having a face-to-face interview instead of a phone conversation. She was silent for several moments. Then she uttered an ''Um'' and a ''well,'' and said, ''I don't know what you mean.''

''David told me that something seemed to be bothering him for close to a year,'' I said, ''and he didn't think it was just the divorce. He was pretty sure it had something to do with Glen Nolte.''

Another long pause. ''It was probably just business,'' she said then, ''but he never talked to me about that stuff.''

''Okay,'' I said. ''Thanks. Just thought I'd ask.''

I said good-bye, made a few notes in my Don file,

and had a breakfast of tea and toast. I was on my second cup of tea when Emily and Janice came in.

"Is Mrs. Gunther here yet?" Janice asked.

"No," I said with a warm smile. "But I'm sure she'll be here soon."

Janice smiled back in the same way. Emily looked from one to the other of us before she took a mug from the cupboard and poured herself some coffee. When Mike arrived a few minutes later, I asked him if he'd like to come along to see Abe Parsons.

"Who is this guy?" he said with a look of disinterest.

"One of Don's childhood friends."

"Any reason to think he's guilty?"

I laughed. "Well, no. Not yet, anyway. He was just a friend. I'm hoping he might know something about Don that someone else wouldn't."

"Naw," Mike said with a wave of his hand. "I think I'll stay here. I have to get the Sherman brief done by tomorrow anyway."

"Okay," I said.

Mrs. Gunther came in a few minutes later, so Janice and I spent almost twenty minutes with her, talking about Erma (no word on her test results yet) and how Mrs. Gunther was getting along. I went to work on my brief after that and didn't stop, even once, until two-fifteen. Then I had a quick half of a peanut butter sandwich on whole-wheat bread, made a cup of tea to drink in the car, and took off to see Abe Parsons.

The day was partly sunny and cool with a bright

blue sky and the most breathtaking clouds. They were full and fluffy, layered with varying shades of gray on the bottom graduating to a nearly luminous white-gold above.

Abe Parsons's office was in West Allis on Burnham Street, only a few miles from where my family lived until we moved to Wauwatosa. There were several maples in front of the store (he was the owner of a small company that sells bathroom fixtures and ceramic tiles) and leaves covered the sidewalk. Most of them had turned a muddy brown but a few bright yellow candidates remained. I picked up a perfect golden leaf, grinned broadly, and put it in my car. When I was a kid, we collected the best ones we could find, placed them in waxed paper lunch bags, and ironed them shut. Then we hung them in the windows. Childhood art. It's still my favorite kind.

When I walked through the door, I saw Abe in the back, deep in conversation with a young man of about twenty. I told the blond woman behind the counter who I was and she walked back and whispered something to Parsons. He turned to look at me, said something to the young man (who then walked away), and came out to greet me.

"Miss Hartley," he said with a smile that looked a little strained. "Come in, please."

I walked around the counter and followed him to a tiny office. It was cluttered and musty, with one tiny window, a ratty-looking couch, and two molded plastic chairs (bright red) in front of a tan metal desk.

Lying on the floor between the two chairs was a sky-blue bathroom sink.

"Please sit down," he said.

We went through the usual preliminary pleasantries and then I got right to the point. "How long did you know Don Balstrum?" I asked.

"Most of my life," he said. "We grew up together. The Balstrums lived two doors away from us."

"So you knew him pretty well?"

"Yes," he said. "I knew him quite well."

"How about as an adult?"

"Once a week, Tuesdays, six-fifteen."

I raised a brow and he smiled. "Workouts at the gym," he said.

"Ah," I said back. "Did you hang out afterward or go right home?"

"We usually grabbed a bite to eat and caught up on the week's events."

"Had you been seeing him lately, like the last few months before his death?"

"Absolutely," Parsons said as he adjusted his shirt collar. "As a matter of fact, I was supposed to meet him the night he was killed. I didn't learn what happened until the next day."

"Did you try to reach him?"

Another shirt-collar adjustment. "I called his office but no one answered."

"Did you leave a message?"

Parsons shook his head. "I didn't see any point. I assumed he'd already left."

"Well, I'm sorry," I said. "It must have been hard to take when you heard what happened."

He nodded and looked away. "Yes, it was."

"I hope you don't mind my asking, but could you give me an idea what Don usually talked about when you were together?"

"I don't mind at all," he said. "We generally talked about business, the news." Then he gave me a shy smile. "And golf. I'm obsessed, according to my wife, and I think even Don agreed. But I just love the game. I get lost in it. It's good therapy." He gave me the same smile again. "I suppose that sounds as farfetched to you as it does to my wife."

"No, not at all. I'm like that myself, about a lot of things. Like knitting. When I first taught myself to knit I didn't want to do anything else. I went nuts."

Parsons laughed and shook his head. "It's good to know I'm not alone," he said, and I smiled. He talked a little more about the game then, figuring, I guess, that he'd found a rare and willing audience. I listened very attentively and gradually moved back to my intended topic.

"Did Don talk about his marriage at all?" I asked when I thought the time was right.

Parsons glanced toward the ceiling and gave me an amused smile. "That was just about all he talked about for well over a year," he said.

"Would you mind telling me what he said?"

Parsons paused and looked thoughtful. "Don didn't handle failure well," he said in a confidential tone.

"And he thought of his divorce as evidence or proof of failure, I believe. From my perspective, it didn't seem like such a bad marriage or even a terribly difficult divorce, but Don took it very hard. He blew everything out of proportion."

"In what way?" I said.

"He focused on the most trivial things—the furniture, the cars, who contributed what to the marriage. I think his profession got in his way, if you want my opinion. He saw Amy as the cause of every difficulty that arose, but from what I could determine, she was pretty darned cooperative."

"Do you know her?" I asked.

"Oh, yes," Parsons said. "Of course, my wife, Justine, knows her best. They play tennis with two other women every Saturday afternoon."

I widened my eyes. "Do you think she'd mind talking to me?"

"I don't see why not," he said.

"How well did she know Don?"

"I'd say if she knows anything about him at all, it's likely she learned it from Amy."

I smiled. "That's exactly what I was hoping you'd say."

Parsons laughed a bit and arched his eyebrows. Then he sat calmly with his hands folded on his desk as if he were patiently waiting for my next question. A most admirable quality in a murder investigation interviewee.

"Did Don act any different recently, say within the last few months?" I asked next.

Abe pursed his lips. "Well, the divorce did have a significant effect on his behavior. He was tense and downright distraught even before they separated. But it would be hard to distinguish that from anything else that might have been bothering him."

"Yeah, I see what you mean," I said. "So you really didn't detect any change or difference that you might attribute to something else?"

Parsons shook his head. "No, I didn't."

"Did he ever complain about anything other than the divorce? Like something to do with his practice, or money problems? Anything like that?"

"He was excessively worried about money as well as his law practice, but my impression was that it was all related to the divorce, though the extent of his concern didn't seem warranted by the circumstances."

"Did he ever ask to borrow money from you?"

Parsons tilted his head to the right and frowned slightly. "No, he didn't, but I would've been surprised if he had. It wasn't something he'd be likely to do."

"Why do you say that?"

"He was too proud," Parsons said with a shrug. "I think he'd find it humiliating to the point where he'd almost have to be desperate to even consider it."

"What if he was desperate? Would he ask you?"

Parsons sighed and squinted at me. "I'd prefer that you keep this between you and me."

I nodded and tried to appear calm.

"I've been experiencing severe cash-flow problems for the last three and a half years and I'm on the verge of filing for bankruptcy. Don was well aware that asking to borrow money from me would have been a wasted effort."

I gave him a sympathetic frown. "Well, I'm sorry to hear that," I said. "I hope things turn out all right for you."

He smiled and nodded a "thank you."

I had a sudden thought. "Did Don ever mention his law partner to you?"

"Well, I knew he had a partner, of course. And I believe he told me he was a good lawyer, but beyond that I don't recall anything particular."

"How about his brother, David?"

"David," he said with a laugh and a shake of his head. "Those two couldn't get along if their lives depended on it. They were at each others' throats from as far back as I can remember."

"What was Don like when you were kids?"

Parsons thought for a few moments. "Well, I guess I'd say he was high-strung. And short-tempered. *Very* angry. He had a great deal to contend with at home. He talked incessantly about running away."

"Did he ever do it?" I said.

"No. I think he was too fearful of the consequences."

"Why did he want to run away? What did he have to put up with that was so difficult?"

Parsons shook his head with a heavy sadness clouding his face. "His father," he said. "That man is a vicious, hateful human being. I truly don't know how they bore it."

"What was he like? How did he treat Don?"

"I'm not sure I can describe this adequately," Parsons said. "To my knowledge, he never physically beat the kids, but the *emotional* abuse. It was tremendous, overwhelming. And I didn't just get this secondhand. I witnessed it myself, time after time." Parsons ran his hand through his hair and actually looked a little sick. "I have never seen such harsh, cruel treatment leveled by an adult against a child. He'd tear into Don—criticize him, hound him, berate him—and he'd keep it up until he had him literally on his knees, sobbing with his head on the floor. He'd tell him he was worthless. He was nothing. Useless. Unwanted. I once heard him say he was the extra they didn't need."

I closed my eyes so tightly it hurt, as if doing so could erase the image from my mind. "How old was he when this happened?" I said.

Parsons looked across the room and stared blankly out the window. "We moved to the neighborhood when I was six. It was going on when I got there and continued until I left for college. For all I know, it started before we arrived."

"So you and Don were the same age?"

Parsons nodded. "We went through grade school and high school together."

I breathed in and out and kept still for close to a minute while Parsons continued to stare out the window.

"How did he do in school?" I said when he appeared ready to talk again.

"Not well," Parsons said. "He acted up a lot, couldn't keep his mind on his work. He was a very sharp guy, don't get me wrong, but he simply couldn't apply himself. He was always getting in trouble."

I'd had quite enough by that point so I decided to end the conversation for the time being. I thanked Parsons as adequately as I could, gave him one of my cards, and left. He looked as relieved to see me go as I was.

I got in my car and sat for a while with a painful lump in my throat, trying not to cry, and trying even harder to get my mind off of Don and his sad, sad childhood. I picked up my maple leaf and turned it over and over, focusing on the yellow color, the graceful movement, the smooth texture. After several minutes had passed and I still wasn't feeling any better, I put the car in gear, drove to the nearest grocery store, and bought some wax-paper bags and a box of Maurice Lenell cookies.

I pulled in the driveway half an hour later, took my leaf and my purchases inside, and went downstairs to put the iron on low. When it was warm enough, I carefully slipped the leaf in a waxed bag, arranged it just the way I wanted it, and sealed it shut. It was perfect, just like the ones I remembered. I turned off the iron, got some tape from my kitchen drawer, and hung my beautiful work of art in the front window. I actually felt better—quite a bit, in fact. It amazes me how such simple, little things can so drastically alter my mood. I have the same experience when a perfect stranger merely smiles at me or says a friendly hello. That tiny gesture of kindness can turn my day from gloom to sunshine in no more than a moment's time. I wished I'd been around to do that for Don when he was a child. The thought came so suddenly that it caught me offguard and I burst into tears.

THE NEXT DAY was Thursday, October 22. At eight-thirty precisely, Mike and I pulled in front of the Balstrums' house in one of the ritziest sections of Fox Point. Mrs. Balstrum answered the door, looked from me to Mike with a slight frown, and asked us to come in. She was very tall, nearly six feet, with large feet and hands and a very big head. Her hair was dark gray, styled in an old-fashioned pageboy. She wore flat, brown leather shoes, a brown wool dress, and a string of pearls. She reminded me of someone but I wasn't sure who. Katharine Hepburn? Nah.

I was about to introduce Mike when he extended his hand, gave her a warm smile, and introduced himself as one of Don's friends from law school. "He was a good law student," Mike said in a kind voice.

"We studied together and he spent a lot of time explaining things to me. He had a good head for tax law."

Mrs. Balstrum watched Mike's face with a hint of a smile. When he'd finished speaking, she said, "Come into the ballroom"—yes, that's what she said—"and sit down."

The room really was an old ballroom with curved windows on the far wall and pale blue wallpaper with a formal dancing scene, the dancers in clothing worn nearly a century ago. In the center of the room was a large antique table, long enough to seat at least sixteen, but there were only six chairs available and none of them matched.

Mrs. Balstrum offered each of us a seat and she sat across from us on the opposite side of the table. Then she looked at Mike and said, "Please, young man, tell me more about Don. I wasn't aware that he had made friends in law school or that he'd put forth much of an effort to do well. I've always believed he was pushed into going."

"Pushed by whom?" I asked. She looked at me as if I'd startled her with my presence and that I was an unwanted intruder.

Mike saw her face and quickly said, "Do you think his brother pushed him into it?"

Mrs. Balstrum turned back to Mike with a smile. "No," she said as if she were considering the possibility. "I don't believe David ever pushed him in that way. It was his father. Arthur has always had very high expectations of the boys.''

Mike nodded and made a face to indicate understanding. ''Then he must have been very proud of Don when he graduated from law school,'' he said.

Mrs. Balstrum sighed and her face took on a far away look. ''I know Don expected him to be,'' she said. ''After all, he'd done what Arthur had asked. But Arthur never offered even a word of congratulations. Instead, he told him he hoped he'd finally measure up to something, like his brother.''

When I let out a little groan, she said, ''I'm sorry, dear. I don't mean to burden you with our family problems.''

Mike smiled. ''It's not a burden to us, Mrs. Balstrum. I came along today because I wanted to meet you and because I wanted an opportunity to talk about Don. I thought it might make his death a little easier for me if I had someone to talk to who really knew him.''

Mrs. Balstrum shook her head and reached across the table for Mike's hand. She had tears in her eyes and kept quiet for a minute, trying to compose herself. Then she said, ''Tell me more about law school. Do you think Don enjoyed it?''

Mike answered that and a dozen more questions and then he started asking questions himself. ''What does Mr. Balstrum do for a living?'' he said.

''He owns and operates three restaurants in Milwaukee,'' Mrs. Balstrum said. ''Buck's Steakhouse,

The Ranch, and Mustang Marvin's." She had a proud look on her face and I smiled.

"I think I've been to Buck's Steakhouse," I said. "It was pretty good, if I remember correctly."

She smiled again. "All of Arthur's restaurants are good. He does very well. He's a hard worker. He always has been."

"What made him decide to go into the restaurant business?" Mike asked.

"Arthur's father ran a restaurant all his life and he left it to Arthur when he died. It was quite successful but it burned down one night. It was determined to be arson but they never caught the arsonists."

Mike shook his head with an expression of disgust. "Did he use the insurance proceeds to buy the next restaurant?" he asked.

Mrs. Balstrum frowned. "I suppose so," she said, looking as if she'd never thought about it before. "Arthur would never talk about the fire. It upset him too much."

Mike looked about to say something but I butted in. "Which restaurant did he buy first, and how soon after that did he acquire the others?" I said.

Mrs. Balstrum raised her eyebrows at me and then frowned with a look of concentration. "Well, I believe he bought Buck's Steakhouse almost immediately—within less than a month, I think. I'm not sure about the others. But I do know that it was no more than three years before he'd acquired them all because

I remember teasing him about buying a new restaurant every year." She laughed a little, so I did, too.

Mike leaned toward her. "Did he ever involve David or Don in his businesses?"

"Oh, yes," Mrs. Balstrum said. "When they were young, Arthur had them bussing and waiting tables, even bartending when they were a little older. It was good for the boys."

"By the way," Mike said, "I was very sorry to hear about Don's divorce. I met his wife when we were in law school and she seemed very nice."

Mrs. Balstrum took a deep breath. "Yes, we were all very sorry about that," she said curtly.

She and Mike talked a while longer and then he stood up to leave so I got up, too. She thanked us for coming and for taking an interest in Don's affairs. She had tears in her eyes when she said good-bye so I told her I'd keep in touch and that seemed to cheer her up.

When we'd pulled out of the driveway and were a few hundred yards down the street, I turned to Mike with a smirk. "You weren't bad back there, Dr. Watson. Where'd you get all that charm?"

Mike shrugged and gave me a half-smile. "I've always had charm," he said. "You just never noticed it." He kept his eyes on me.

I smiled and then laughed a little. "Well," I said. "What did you think? What was it you'd planned to ask her, by the way? You said you had some questions you already knew you wanted to ask."

"I wanted to know about the old man's business," Mike said. "I remembered when you were talking to Chuck Barker that Don and I had talked about it once."

"What did he say?"

"Very little," Mike said with emphasis. "I asked him what his father did and he was reluctant to talk about it. He told me he ran a few restaurants but I had to practically drag the names out of him, and when I asked him if he ever considered going into the restaurant business himself, he changed the subject. It just struck me as odd so I thought it was worth looking into."

"Maybe I should ask David about it," I said. "And I haven't talked to Mr. Balstrum yet. You want to come with me when I do?"

Mike laughed. "You bet I do," he said. "That's one interview I don't want to miss."

As soon as we got home, I pulled out the yellow pages and dialed Buck's Steakhouse.

"He's at Mustang today," said the young woman who answered, and she gave me the number.

"Arthur Balstrum here. How may I help you?" he said when he finally picked up (it took nearly ten minutes).

I identified myself and gave him the really quick version of what I was doing.

"I've got two parties going today and tomorrow's

one of our busiest nights," he said. "How about tomorrow morning? I'll be here at seven a.m."

"That would be great, Mr. Balstrum. Thank you very much." He actually sounded like a reasonably pleasant person, which certainly came as a surprise after the descriptions I'd received.

I went into the library to find Mike. "I just talked to Arthur Balstrum," I told him with a look of amazement, "and he readily agreed to talk to me at seven tomorrow morning. He actually seemed *nice*."

"He's hiding something," Emily said and went back to her work.

I grinned and winked at Mike. "You're probably right," I said.

Mike creased his brow. "Did you say seven a.m.?"

I shrugged. "I can't get too picky about time with these people. They don't have to talk to me in the first place, you know."

Mike grunted. "Okay, I'll be there. Meet you here at six-thirty."

FRIDAY, OCTOBER 23. At 6:40 a.m., Mike and I were on our way to Mustang Marvin's on Oakland Avenue.

"What's he doing at a restaurant in the middle of the night?" Mike asked me in an edgy voice.

"It's not the middle of the night," I said, "and he's probably just doing paperwork or getting ready to open. If you really want to know, just ask him."

"Maybe I will," he said.

"What're you doing here in the middle of the

night?'' Mike said to Balstrum as soon as he opened the door for us.

I rolled my eyes while Balstrum peered at Mike through bifocal lenses resting halfway down his nose. He was about six feet tall with a slight, wiry build and medium brown hair thinned significantly on top. He didn't give Mike an answer.

''Come in,'' he said to me. I followed him through a dark dining room decorated in red with an equestrian theme—saddles and such suspended from a beamed ceiling, riding equipment, and photographs of horses hanging on the walls.

''What kind of food do you serve here?'' I asked, but immediately regretted it since I knew I'd given away that I'd never been there.

''Steaks,'' Mike said. ''Good ones.'' We both looked at him in surprise and Balstrum had an amused smile on his face. ''Glad you like them,'' he said to Mike.

Mike shrugged and kept walking. We stopped at a little office down a hallway between the dining room and the kitchen.

''I'll try not to take too much time,'' I said after he'd cleared some papers from two chairs that were against one wall. He pulled them out and placed them in front of his desk. Mike and I sat down but Balstrum remained standing.

''I'm trying to find out what was going on in Don's life before he was killed and I was hoping you could help me,'' I said.

Balstrum looked down at me through the bifocals, little rectangular lenses with golden wire rims. "Far as I know," he said, "he was busy practicing law."

"How extensively was Don involved in your restaurant business?" Mike blurted out.

Balstrum leaned against the desk and glared at Mike. It was a controlled glare and looked like it took some effort. He didn't answer so Mike repeated the question. Balstrum walked behind the desk, sat down, and looked at me. "Do you have anymore questions?" he asked.

I held my breath for a few moments. "Is there some reason why you can't answer Mike's question?" I said in the most unconfrontational voice I could manage.

Balstrum sucked in his cheeks, glared at me for a few moments, and said, "I tried to involve the boys in the business from the time they were young. I gave Don some legal work from time to time after he graduated from law school."

"What about David?" I said. "Has he ever done any legal work for you?"

Balstrum hesitated a moment before he shook his head. "He wasn't interested. Too busy."

"Your father ran your first restaurant when you were growing up, your wife told us."

"Yes," Balstrum said.

"I'm sorry about the fire. That must have been hard to take."

Balstrum's expression was cold and he made no response.

"You're doing well now, though, Mrs. Balstrum said."

"Yes. Quite well."

I was trying my best to ignore his relentless, hard look—very much like David's, I realized later. I sighed, looked over at Mike, and sighed again. I was just about to say something when Mike took over.

Mike asked Balstrum the usual questions regarding Don's recent behavior, whether anything seemed to be bothering him and all that sort of thing. Balstrum barely said anything until Mike reached the topic of Don's divorce.

"Do you have any idea what caused them to break up?" he asked.

"The first I knew anything was the day they announced their divorce," Balstrum snapped.

"Do you know if he discussed it with anyone else in the family?" I asked.

Balstrum formed his lips into an expression of distaste. "You might ask David," he said. "I came home early one day and Amy was at the house with him."

"They were at *your* house?" Mike said, and Balstrum nodded.

"Was it on a weekend?" I asked.

"Middle of the week," Balstrum said.

"Was your wife there?"

He shook his head.

"What were they doing there?" Mike said.

Balstrum waved the back of his hand in our direction. "I have no idea. David said he'd come to pick up some documents or some such hogwash."

"And you didn't believe him?" I said.

Balstrum pursed his lips. "No, I did not. I could tell they were up to something the moment I walked in."

"Were Amy and David close friends?" Mike asked.

Balstrum shook his head. "As far as I knew, they rarely saw each other."

"Did they look like they'd been arguing?"

Balstrum looked thoughtful for a moment. "No," he said. "At least...well, I'm not sure. Amy did seem upset."

"How soon was this before the divorce?" I asked.

"Oh, it was after the divorce," Balstrum said. "It was just last month."

"SO WHAT DID you think?" I asked Mike as we were driving home.

He shrugged, stuffed his hands in the pockets of his jacket, and pressed one of his untied, high-top-sneaker-clad feet against my dashboard.

"Strange dude," he said.

"Yeah, very strange. What did you make of that story about David and Amy?"

Mike guffawed. "That was a real hoot. Think they have something going?"

I scrunched up my face. "No way. She's not the type."

"Everybody's the type," Mike said.

I gave him a reproachful look. "That's absolutely not true," I said.

When we were back at the house, I offered to make breakfast and Mike accepted. We were still hanging out in the kitchen when Janice and Emily arrived. After the three of them went to the library, I gave David a call at his office.

"Beth, how can I help you?" he said in a frazzled voice.

"I can tell you're really busy so I won't keep you, but I was hoping we could get together within the next few days. I have something I really need to talk to you about."

He sighed heavily. "Okay, sure," he said. "I'm sorry, I'm up against a lot of deadlines today. I feel like I have a dozen forest fires to put out and I just ran out of water."

"I know the feeling," I said with a laugh.

He laughed, too, though his was pretty strained. "I'll tell you what. Why don't we get together tonight? Maybe we could go to dinner. As a matter of fact, I was thinking of hiring you. Do you do anything other than briefs?"

"Not usually," I said. "I've done a few memoranda but that's a rare request. Why? What did you have in mind?"

"I'm not even sure," he said. "Why don't we talk about it tonight? Can I pick you up?"

"It might be better to meet somewhere," I said. "I told my parents I might stop by their house tonight so it'd be easier if I have my car."

"Okay, sure, that's fine," he said. "How about Jake's on North Avenue, say seven-thirty?"

"That's fine," I said. "I'll see you then."

I was still in the kitchen when Mrs. Gunther arrived (at least an hour after her usual time). She was moving very slowly again. Her hair was a mess and she wore no makeup at all, though usually she wears quite a lot.

"Are you all right?" I said, knowing, of course, that she wasn't.

She let out a long sigh and lowered herself to a chair. "I'm holding up," she said, "but it's taking its toll."

I gave her a look of sympathy and concern. "Have you had anymore news?"

"Not yet," she said. She ran her right hand through her hair and it looked worse than ever. "It's the waiting that does it. It's the hardest part. I'd rather have the news than put up with the waiting."

"I know what you mean," I said. "Once you know, you can at least start to deal with it."

She gave me a fond smile and I smiled back. I made her a cup of tea and some toast and talked with her while she ate. When she said she was ready to get to work, I went into the library and did the same.

I hadn't been working nearly hard enough since I'd gotten involved in Don's case so I kept going until almost three-thirty, when I was too hungry to think straight.

I went to the kitchen, made myself a peanut butter sandwich on whole wheat (a recent addiction), and added some notes to my Don file as I ate. I really needed to talk to Abe Parsons's wife, Justine. And I wanted to ask David about his father's restaurant business and Don's involvement. I could take care of that when I saw him at dinner that night, so I thought I'd give Justine a call. Abe had given me her work number. I decided to try that first and was put on hold while I listened to WOKY over the telephone.

"Justine Parsons here," she answered a few minutes later.

I introduced myself, explained why I was calling, and told her how I'd gotten her number. She didn't hesitate for a moment.

"I *never* betray the confidences of my friends," she said. "If there's anything you need to know about Amy Balstrum you can ask her yourself."

"It's really Don I want to know about," I said.

"You can ask Amy," Justine said again. "It's none of my affair." She hung up.

I sat for ten minutes, doodling and fuming. I know I don't have the right to expect anyone to talk to me but I've sort of gotten used to them generally responding in a positive way. And I'm stubborn so I wasn't giving up. I called back.

"If I get Amy's permission first, will you talk to me then?" I said.

Justine paused before she answered. "Well...maybe. But have her call *me* and tell me it's okay. I want to be sure there's no misunderstanding here."

I rolled my eyes. "Okay, I will."

As soon as we hung up, I dialed Amy's work number and was told she was busy with a patient. I left a message asking her to call as soon as she could.

Forty-five minutes later, she called me back and sounded a bit worried. When I explained the situation, she laughed uneasily and asked why I needed to talk to Justine rather than her directly.

"Only because it's useful to get another person's perspective on something. People usually see and remember things differently."

When Amy didn't respond, I said, "It was my idea to ask your permission, not Justine's. There's nothing weird going on, really. If you feel uncomfortable about it, I won't talk to her. It's not that important. It's just that sometimes I learn things this way that I otherwise wouldn't."

She still didn't answer and I was about to give up when she said, "Okay. I suppose I don't mind. I guess I just felt like you were suspecting me of something."

I assured her that I wasn't, thanked her profusely, and asked her to please call Justine and then call me right back.

Fifteen minutes later, my phone rang again, but it

was Justine rather than Amy. "I'll talk to you," she said, "but it has to be on my terms."

"That's perfectly fine," I said as I wrinkled my nose at the phone.

"Can you come by tomorrow between four and four-thirty?"

"Sure," I said. "Just tell me where."

After she'd given me directions and hung up, I made some notes in the Don file regarding both Justine's and Amy's reactions. Both were acting a little strange, I thought. Too nervous. Too worried. Too guarded. Then again, it was a murder investigation and the victim's spouse (not to mention ex-spouse) is always a prime suspect. Who wouldn't be a bit anxious under the circumstances?

I sat back and looked out the window as leaves tumbled from the trees, a free-floating foliage ballet performed just for me. I smiled to myself and thought about my upcoming interviews. I was seeing David that night and Justine the next afternoon. I'm still not sure which one I ultimately found most enlightening.

SIX

I ARRIVED AT JAKE'S at seven-twenty and spotted David already seated at a table, gulping a martini with three olives in it. As I walked toward him, he removed one of the olives from a toothpick and ate it with a suggestive smirk aimed directly at me. Alcohol dribbled down his chin. I pretended not to notice. I sat down, said hello, and looked over the menu while David looked over me. I pretended not to notice that, either.

"So you're overloaded at work, huh?" I said.

He looked skyward and snorted a laugh. "Now there's an understatement," he said.

"How many people do you have working with you?"

"There are four of us altogether. My partner, Clem Bailey, myself, and two associates. The trouble is, I've gotten so busy that I've been monopolizing the associates and it's been creating some problems for Clem. He relies on them for most of his research and writing, even some of the investigating."

"So what happened? Did you get a lot of new business recently?"

"No more than usual, but I have three trials to

prepare for in the next four weeks and I've been just a bit overwrought since Don's death.''

I gave him a sympathetic look. "I can certainly understand that," I said.

After the waitress took our orders, I said, "I know I've asked you this before, but how close were you and Amy?"

"We weren't close at all," he said. "I never cared for her much," he added with an expression of distaste.

"I talked to your father today. He told me he saw you and Amy talking at his house about a month ago. What was that all about?"

David looked at me rather sharply and didn't answer.

"He told us he came home early one day and you and Amy were at the house, and when he asked you what you were doing there, you told him you came to pick up some papers. But why was Amy there?"

"I don't know what she was doing there," David said. His voice was raised to an embarrassing level and he had such a tight hold on his martini glass that I was afraid it would break. A man and woman two tables away turned and looked at us and David saw me notice them. He clenched his jaw and stared back at them, and continued staring even after they'd turned around.

In a moment, he turned back to me and said, "What was that, now?"

"Why was Amy there?" I said.

David took a deep breath and pursed his lips. "She told me she stopped by to see my mother. I said she wasn't there but I asked her to come in anyway. To be polite. She left when my father came and I left shortly after that."

I nodded. It sounded plausible enough, but then why was he so upset?

"Do you know why Don and Amy broke up?" I said.

"Beth, you've asked me this before. I told you I don't know. Why don't you ask Amy? I'm sure she'll have a scintillating distortion of the facts for you. It's a rare person who'll admit when something is entirely their fault."

"Why do you think it was entirely her fault? It's probably never entirely one person's fault."

"It was in this case," he muttered.

A strangely stubborn and unyielding attitude for someone claiming to know absolutely nothing about it. I just let it go. I tried to make small talk for a while until I thought he'd calmed down. When he was smiling again, I said, "You know, I'd really like a chance to get a look at Don's house. Would you mind terribly if I did that?"

He frowned and thought for a few moments. "I don't see why not," he said. "I have the keys. I could take you through myself."

"Could you do it tonight?"

"No. Tonight's not good for me. How about if I

let you know. I'll give you a call within the next few days.''

"Okay," I said. "That'll be fine. I know you're really busy."

He smiled and nodded a few times. "Speaking of which," he said, "would you be available to write a brief and a couple of memos for me within the next couple of weeks?"

"Absolutely," I said. "But I have to warn you I won't necessarily be able to do all of them personally. So long as you're willing to let Mike Shepard or Emily Schaeffer handle what I can't get to, I'm sure we can fit them in."

He frowned. "Well, I'd prefer you. But I'll accept that if it's my only choice."

"Okay. Why don't you call me when you get the chance and give me the details."

"I'll call you first thing tomorrow morning," he said. Then he leaned back and narrowed his eyes. "You're quite pleasant to be with, do you know that? You have a very calming effect on people."

"Thanks," I said, giving him an awkward smile. Then I quickly changed the subject. "By the way, what can you tell me about Don's involvement in your father's restaurants?"

David's face reddened and he became very still.

"David?" I said.

Still no response.

"Do you know anything about it?"

He took a deep breath and slowly released it. "No," was all he said.

"Are you aware that Don gave your father legal advice from time to time?"

David stiffened again and gave me a hard, cold look. "What of it?" he said.

I shrugged. "Didn't he want to practice with you when he got out of law school?"

David swallowed hard before answering my question. "Yes, but I didn't need anyone at the time."

"Why was he doing part-time work for your father? Doesn't your dad already have an attorney?"

"Of course he does. What of it? And what possible significance can any of this have to my brother's death?"

"I don't know," I said with a shrug. Then I had a sudden thought—a thought I decided to keep to myself. David wasn't the person to ask but either Cassandra or Amy, or even Laney, might very well have the answer.

"One more question," I said. "Did you ever meet Laney Shaw?"

David's eyebrows met. "No, I never met her, but I know of her. She and Don were good friends. I think it could have developed into something more serious over time, but according to Don, neither of them wanted to get involved in another relationship so soon."

"And you believed him?" I said.

"Sure," David said. "Why wouldn't I?"

I ended the inquisition at that point and we talked about other things—David's hobbies, his children, a little about Cassandra—and then we went home. I offered very politely to call him a cab, given his intake of alcohol, but he declined.

It was nearly ten when I pulled in my driveway. I was just about to get out of my car when something stopped me. I had the distinct impression that something was wrong. Something was different. I stayed in the car and looked around but I couldn't see a thing. It was then that I realized my neighbor's security lights were off, and they're always on at that time of night even when they're out of town. I told myself I was being silly but I had such a strong sense that someone was out there, covered by darkness, that I had to force myself to get out and go inside. I locked the car, left it in the driveway under my carport, and bolted the door as soon as I got in the house. My heart was pounding and I was breathing fast. I told myself over and over again that I was just imagining things—there couldn't have been anyone out there— but for some reason I was never entirely convinced.

THE NEXT DAY was Saturday, October 24. David called me at 11:00 a.m. and did a quick run-through of the cases he wanted help with. We agreed that I would stop by his office later that day to pick up the files.

I went grocery shopping and bought everything I needed for my dinner with Mrs. Robinson, walked up and down my stairs eighty-five times (I hurt my foot jumping rope), took another shower, and then headed for David's law office across from the Peck Pavilion.

We'd arranged for me to call before I left so he was waiting for me in the lower lobby when I arrived. He let me in and we took the elevator, David staring at me the whole ride up while I stared at the floor. When we reached his office, he dropped himself onto his chair and gave me an anxious smile. "I am so glad you're here," he said. "I can't tell you how much I appreciate this."

"That's quite all right," I said. "One of the purposes of my business is to help people during overload times. I'm glad I can do it."

David had rings of sweat under his arms and his hair was damp. For someone purportedly so successful, he certainly seemed to have a tremendous amount of difficulty handling the stresses of his job. He smiled again and this time it was a little more relaxed. "I enjoyed our dinner last night," he said.

I averted my eyes. "So did I. Now why don't you show me the files you want me to work on."

We went through everything he felt was relevant, passing papers across the desk, and then he handed the whole lot to me and sat back in his chair with a strange smirk on his face.

"Now then, have you made any progress on the case?"

"Not really," I said, feeling a bit confused since we'd just discussed that the night before. "I feel like the more people I talk to the more confused I become.''

He laughed and sat up a bit straighter.

''I realize you're a bit overwhelmed here, but have you given any thought to when I could look through Don's house?''

''Yes, as a matter of fact, I was just thinking about that before you arrived. What is it you expect to find, if I might ask?''

''Nothing in particular,'' I said. ''I just want to take a look. You never know, something might just trigger an idea, but I won't know that until I see it.''

He nodded. ''How about tomorrow afternoon, say around two? I could meet you there.''

I raised my eyebrows. ''Sure,'' I said. ''That'd be great.''

IT WAS ALMOST three-thirty when I got home so I had just enough time to have a carton of yogurt and a cup of tea before I left for Justine's. Justine lived on Twenty-seventh Street, a few blocks south of Burnham (very near her husband's store). The house was a honey-colored brick with dark green trim and a brown front door. I rang the bell and looked up and down the block as I waited. I've always liked that neighborhood. The houses have so much character and each one has its own unique charm. In fact, now that I think of it, there are some Frank Lloyd Wright houses only a few blocks away.

Justine answered the door with a strained smile and

asked me to come in. The interior was dark and the rooms were small. A hallway led directly to the kitchen which could be seen from the front door, and the living-room was off to the left. I didn't see a dining room.

She walked straight to the living-room couch and sat down without a word, so I took a seat in the nearest chair (there were only two) and willed myself to be at ease, which wasn't easy given the hostile look on her face.

"Well," I said. "I really do appreciate this. I know it's an inconvenience and I'll try to keep it short."

Same look, no response. Great beginning.

"Mrs. Parsons," I said. "I talked to Amy and she assured me it was all right with her if I talked to you. She's already told me everything she could think of that might help and we agreed that you might just remember something she'd forgotten."

Justine's shoulders relaxed and she shifted her position. Then she sighed and leaned against the back of the couch. "Okay," she said, as if attempting to apologize without having to actually *say* it. "What can I help you with?"

"I was wondering if you can remember any of the details of the problems Don was having with his law partner," I said. Amy had flatly denied knowing anything about it but I was trying to make it appear to Justine that Amy and I had actually discussed it. It worked a lot better than I'd expected.

Justine raised an eyebrow. "You mean the trouble with the money?" she said.

Talk about hitting a jackpot. I tried to look as casual and calm as possible. "Right," I said. "Can you remember anything about that?"

She opened a palm and shrugged. "There wasn't much to it, from what I can recall. Don's partner was embezzling money from the clients but he was trying to put it off on Don."

"You mean Glen was trying to make it look like Don was the one embezzling the money," I said as if I'd heard it all before.

"Right. Anyway, I do know that Glen never got caught and I think Don threatened to turn him in at one point but he never went through with it. Then Glen ended up threatening to turn Don in, if you can believe that. Of all the nerve. Can you imagine?"

I shook my head in feigned disgust. "When did Amy first tell you about this?"

Justine scrunched up her face. "I think it was about five or six months ago."

I stared at her for a few moments and thought carefully about how to phrase my next question. "You know, it just occurred to me that I never thought to ask Amy this, but why would Don have told her about that when they were just about to get divorced?"

"Because he was frightened to death it would come out during the divorce," Justine said. "He was afraid that her attorney's attempt to get part of his law practice for her would result in the discovery of the embezzlement. He actually offered her money on the sly to get him to back off.''

"Did she go along with it?'' I asked with a look of surprise I couldn't hold back.

"Certainly, she went along with it. She's no fool. She made an easy five grand. Of course, it wasn't as much as she would've gotten if she'd received a share of his practice but she didn't want any part of that after she learned about the embezzlement. She was afraid she'd get accused of something herself if she acquired an interest in it. I thought she was being a little paranoid, myself, but what could I say?''

I nodded, my mind racing as I tried to appear cool. I can just imagine what I really looked like. I wanted to ask more but I was afraid of revealing that this was the first time I'd heard the story so I decided to drop it for then. I asked Justine several additional questions about things Amy and I really had discussed but I didn't learn anything new so I stood to leave.

"Thank you so much for your time,'' I told Justine as I held out my hand. She shook it and gave me a self-conscious smile.

"You're welcome,'' was all she said.

I drove home with a big grin on my face. I wasn't sure, of course, if either Don or Glen really had been guilty of embezzlement, but if either of them had, they'd both have a significant interest in covering it up.

THAT NIGHT, Brian picked me up at eight, took me to dinner at Cafe Marché, and to a nightclub to listen to music. While we ate, he smiled fondly at me at least a thousand times and talked nonstop about his cases (something he rarely does) and everything that was going on with me. He wanted to know how Mrs. Robinson was doing, what she thought about the Balstrum case, and what I thought so far. He wasn't sarcastic or defensive when he asked and he responded in a sincere and equable manner to everything I said.

When I told him I was going to be shown through Don's house the next day, he said, "We've already searched it, of course, but I'll be interested in your opinion." I gave him a doubtful look and he said, "I know I haven't given you reason to believe that in the past but I have a different attitude now. I really do want to know what you think." When I wrinkled my brow, he said, "Beth, I'm telling you the truth. I admit it took me a long time to accept, but you solved two murders and you did it without any significant help from the department. That's pretty darned impressive. You are the hottest topic at the station, you know."

I opened my eyes wide. "I am?" I said.

"Yes, you are," he said with a big grin.

I laughed and gave him a mischievous smirk. "Did *you* find anything at Don's house?"

"Yes, but you know I can't share those things with you."

I pretended to pout.

"Beth," he said.

"I know, I'm just kidding. I'll just have to work with whatever I can find on my own."

He smiled approvingly but I detected a bit of wariness. It occurred to me just then to tell him what I'd learned from Justine but I wasn't sure I wanted to let go of that little tidbit quite yet.

We stayed at the nightclub for nearly two hours and then Brian took me home and stayed another hour and a half. He talked about things he wanted us to do together and many of them were to take place rather far into the future. He hugged me incessantly, kept touching my face and holding my hand. When he left, I was ridiculously in love and hungry as I could be. I had two scoops of butter pecan ice cream and then precooked my dinner for Mrs. Robinson since I was too wired up to sleep.

I baked a cherry pie, made a pot roast with beef, carrots, potatoes, green beans, and onions, and got out my Bisquick mix so I wouldn't forget it (she loves baking powder biscuits). By the time I was done, it was nearly midnight and I was exhausted but still wide awake. I did a little knitting, then a little reading, and finally went to bed at 2:00 a.m.

I HEARD THE RUSTLE of leaves, something brush against a bush, and I looked every which way, straining to see in the darkness. Then I heard him behind me. I turned and tried to scream at the man without a face. I tried again but no sound came out. He was reaching

for me, grasping, moving closer and closer. But I
couldn't scream. I couldn't move.

I WOKE UP in a cold sweat, my whole body trembling
with fear. I barely slept at all for the rest of the night.

SUNDAY, OCTOBER 25. I called Emily and asked her
if she was still up for having breakfast (she'd left a
message on my machine the day before, suggesting
it).

"Sure," she said. "You want to just meet at Ma
Fisher's?"

We agreed to be there at eleven so I showered and
dressed, grabbed my Don file, and left for Farwell
Avenue. Emily was already there when I arrived, sitting in a booth along the east wall.

"What'd you bring that for?" she asked when she
saw my file.

"I don't know, I just thought you might want to
know about the investigation. You got pretty interested in the last one."

She nearly sneered. "I wasn't *interested*," she said.
"I was just trying to find out how much trouble you
were getting yourself into."

I rolled my eyes. "Well, are you interested in how
much trouble I'm getting into *this* time?"

She laughed weakly but didn't say anything.

"I really like hearing your opinion on this stuff,"
I said. "You came up with some pretty good ideas
on Dave's case, you know."

She looked across the room. "You have Mike helping you now. What do you need me for?"

So that was it. "Mike may be helping me," I said, "but I still want to know what you think. You have good ideas. You might help me think of something."

She let a faint smile escape and looked back at me. Then she shrugged and said, "Okay, what's going on so far?"

I gave her the gist of all the interviews I'd done by referring to my notes.

"What about Laney?" Emily said. "Do you think she could've done it?"

"Laney?" I said. "No way. They were friends. Why would she kill him?"

"So she says. Maybe they were more than friends. And maybe he dumped her and she paid him back."

I shook my head. "No way," I said. "I don't believe that."

"Well, how about this?" Emily said. "What if he was embezzling money from her?"

My eyes opened wide. "Oh, my gosh," I said. "I never thought of that."

You should've seen the self-satisfied grin on Emily's face. I smiled back. "Good work, Sherlock. You see why I ask for your help?"

This time her smile was brimming with appreciation and warmth.

We each had another cup of decaf, talked a while longer, and went back to my place until I had to leave for Don's house.

The house was in Wauwatosa and I'd been surprised to find out that he'd lived only five blocks from my parents. It was set back from the street and two large oaks and a gingko tree took up a major portion of the front yard. The facade was red brick, there were two stories, and the roof looked in need of some repair. The trim was newly painted, though, and the grounds were well kept. David's shiny black BMW was parked out front so I rang the bell. He answered a few moments later and led me through a small papered foyer (dark green with a narrow rust stripe) with brass fixtures. The living room had hunter green wall-to-wall carpeting, oak furniture, a collection of duck and hunting prints, and blond-paneled walls. A couch, two easy chairs, and a love seat were upholstered in a coarse taupe fabric with green, beige, and rust throw pillows in assorted prints and stripes, all perfectly co-ordinated. David waited while I walked around the room. There were no photographs, papers or clutter of any kind. Everything was neat and clean.

The dining room was papered to match the foyer. The dining table was oak, seated six, and matched the small hutch set against one of the walls. This time the artwork was oil paintings, everyone an original from what I could see. On the floor beneath the wall of paintings were three cardboard boxes.

"Do you know what's in those boxes?" I asked him.

He looked at me with a hint of a smile. "Yes, but I'll bet you want to take a look yourself."

I laughed. "I sure do, if you don't mind."

"Be my guest," he said.

The first box contained odds and ends that looked like junk most people would've discarded already: an old paperweight with a missing piece, some stained kitchen towels, the head of a golf club, and a hard cover book without the front cover. The next box was a little more interesting. It held legal documents from files Don must have worked on at sometime. I carefully looked through them but nothing awakened my suspicion. The third box was filled with old paperbacks, mostly suspense and spy novels.

David showed me the den after that. It was carpeted in gold with a worn brown couch, a TV and VCR, a stereo and CD player, a rowing machine, an indoor putting tray, and a set of golf clubs. A floor-to-ceiling bookcase took up an entire wall. He had at least three shelves full of videotapes, a full shelf of CDs, reference books of every kind, travel catalogs, dozens of photo albums, magazines, and a large collection of history and war-related books. There was a pile of newspapers on the floor at one end of the couch. That was it. An awful lot of stuff, but nothing worth bothering with as far as I was concerned.

The kitchen was adjacent to the den, painted a light gold, with orange, green, and gold wallpaper with a rooster motif above the chair rail. I looked in the refrigerator (don't ask me why) and found a carton of eggs, a quart of orange juice, a bag of apples, lunch meat of some sort, cheese, and margarine.

I consented to being shown the bathrooms after that, though I was pretty sure they would yield no clues either, and then the bedrooms, three in all. The first one had been converted to a weight room, with a bench, a full set of free weights, and a Universal machine. The second was obviously used as Don's bedroom. There was nothing in the closet but clothing and the same was true for the chest of drawers.

The third bedroom had been converted to an office and contained a desk, a computer, file cabinets, and bookcases. I asked David if I could look through the desk and file cabinet and check the computer files.

"I already tried the computer," he said, "but he used a password for everything and I haven't been able to figure it out. You're welcome to search everything else, though. I'll be in the kitchen if you need me. Can I bring you something to drink?"

"No thanks," I said. When he left the room I opened the top drawer of the file cabinet, removed the files, and put them on the desk. I sat down in the swivel chair and opened the first in the pile. Charge-card bills. I carefully read each one and found nothing the least bit suspicious—just grocery stores, filling stations, a Nissan dealership, The Boston Store, Sears, Marshall Field's, Circuit City, and the like. There were five files remaining in the pile and each one was as uninteresting as the last. I was feeling pretty disappointed when David walked in. "Find anything helpful?" he said.

"Not so far," I said with a sigh.

He gave me an indecipherable look and left the room. I opened the middle drawer. It contained only three files. One held the documents for the closing of Don's house. I scanned them but nothing looked out of the ordinary. The next contained insurance documents, the one after that, medical bills. I looked them over, put everything back, and opened the bottom drawer. It was empty. I sighed, closed the drawer, and started searching the desk. I found the usual assortment of pens and pencils, paper clips, a stapler, a few pads of paper, and some mailing labels—and that was it. I spent another fifteen minutes trying to come up with Don's computer password and then I told David I was ready to go home. A total waste of time. What annoyed me the most was the fact that I'd have to tell Brian I hadn't found anything—and I was sure he'd ask.

"Why did Don want to stay here after the divorce?" I asked David as we were walking out. "Isn't it kind of big for just one person?"

David sighed. "Yes," he said. "I suppose it is. But Don renovated this house and he did all the work himself. It took him almost five years. It was a part of him. He didn't want to give it up." He looked at me sideways. "I'll bet you think that's syrupy and sentimental, don't you?"

"Not at all," I said. "Not one bit. I think I'd feel the same way."

He awarded me a smile that actually had some warmth to it.

I told David good-bye, went home, changed my clothes, and left immediately for Mrs. Robinson's. Though I felt rushed and harried because of all my activity, we still had a wonderful time. Our after-dinner talk lasted even longer than usual, and when I got home that night, I felt secure, for some reason, that I was safe and alone. No evil interlopers hiding in the night. No one watching. No one waiting. I put the car in the garage, went inside, and slept soundly until morning. I didn't know it then, of course, but it would be quite sometime before I'd enjoy such serenity again.

SEVEN

It was Monday, October 26, 11:03 a.m., and the mailman was at my front door. Now, I don't want you to think that I'm afraid of my mailman. And I'm certainly not afraid of mail, per se. But since that day, there are certain sounds and sights associated with the U.S. Postal Service that evoke some very unsettling responses.

That morning, along with the usual assortment of bills, letters, and Victoria's Secret catalogs, I received a large envelope. It was brown, nine by twelve, and it was addressed with letters cut from a magazine. At first, I thought it was a joke and I laughed as I opened the envelope. Inside was a glossy black-and-white photograph—a photograph of me doing something I'd never realized anyone had witnessed. I was standing outside Abe Parsons's store, picking up a yellow maple leaf. By itself, the photo didn't strike me as particularly threatening. But the note did. It, too, was fashioned from magazine letters and the message was short and simple: *STiLL aLIve?*

I sat on my couch, tried to calm myself, and read it again. I had to call Brian, there was no way around it.

"I'll be right over," he said.

He was there in ten minutes, which meant he had to have driven way over the speed limit. He *never* drives that fast when I'm with him. Once, I literally begged him to take me for a ride in his unmarked car with the siren going and the cherry on top but he absolutely refused.

"Let me see it," he said the moment I let him in. He held both the photograph and the letter by the very edges as he always does and as I never do because I can't seem to remember. When he saw me wince, he said, "You got your fingerprints all over everything, didn't you?"

"I'm sorry," I said. I gave him a sheepish smile and tried to look cute but I don't think it worked.

He shook his head and made a face meant to indicate disappointment but it was sort of good-natured at the same time. "Do you know when this was taken?" he said.

"Yes, I can look it up. I keep a file on all my interviews. Hold on a minute.

"It was Wednesday, October twenty-first, a little before three o'clock," I said when I returned with my Don file.

Brian looked very impressed and didn't try to hide it. "Good going," he said. "You're very meticulous. That's a valuable trait in this line of work."

I gave him a modest smile. He stayed a while longer, kissed me good-bye, and took the photo and letter with him. After he'd left, I remembered I hadn't told him about my fear that someone had been waiting for me in the dark after I'd had dinner with David the other night, but after I thought about it I decided it was better not to. He'd just get even more concerned for my safety and start giving me a hard time. That was the last thing I needed.

When I told Janice, Emily, and Mike about my mail, Emily asked who I'd talked to before the picture was taken.

I gave her an appreciative nod. "That's exactly what I was about to find out. It's all in my notes."

I opened the Don file and ticked off the names. "Okay, I'd seen Laney Shaw, Glen Nolte, Amy, Amy's lawyer, Don's brother, his sister, Chuck Barker...and that's it. Oh, and I'd met Abe Parsons, Cassandra, and Mrs. Balstrum at the wake."

"Viewing," Mike said.

"Whatever."

"That's an awful lot of people," Janice said, "and it could be any one of them."

"Yep, and it could also be someone who learned from one of those people that I was involved in the investigation."

"Oh, wow," Janice said. "That could be anybody."

I nodded in agreement.

TUESDAY, OCTOBER 27. At nine-ten, I called Don's office and asked the receptionist if I could speak to Don's secretary if she was still working there. She hesitated a moment and asked me to wait. Glen took the call.

"Beth," he said. "What can I do for you?"

I was dying to ask him about the embezzlement right then and there but I wasn't prepared so I forced myself to wait. "Well, nothing," I said in response to his question. "I called to talk to Don's secretary. She was the one I asked for."

"What do you want to speak with her about?"

"I'd like to talk to her about Don," I said pleasantly. "I don't know why I didn't think of it before. She's certainly someone who would know his personality. She might have detected a change in his behavior before his death."

Glen hesitated a bit. "Okay," he said. "I'll put you through. But it has to be on her own time. I really can't spare her during office hours. We're so overloaded since his death I can't even see straight."

"Yeah, I'll bet," I said. "Thanks, Glen."

I heard a few clicks and then a woman said, "This is Miss Andrews."

I introduced myself and asked if she'd mind talking with me about Don, perhaps over dinner, my treat.

"Oh, not at all," she said. "I'm free tonight after six but tomorrow night is my bowling league and Thursdays I go see my aunt, so it'll have to be either tonight or maybe Friday, if that works for you." She spit all of that out in one breath.

"Tonight would be wonderful," I said. "I'll even pick you up if you want."

"No, you don't have to do that. I have my own car. We could just meet somewhere. I live near UWM."

"Then you're right near me," I said. "What kind of food do you like?"

"Anything. I'm not picky."

"How about the Coffee Trader? It's near both of us and there's never a long wait."

"Perfect," she said. "Would six-thirty be all right?"

"Just fine. I'll see you there." I had a feeling I was going to like Miss Andrews.

I made myself another cup of tea, brought it into the library, and got to work. But I kept watching the clock, ticking away the minutes. I was waiting for my mail.

At 11:15 a.m., I heard him. My mailman, mild-mannered Mr. Porter, opened my letter box and my heart started to race. I took a deep breath, waited until I was certain he was gone, and went to retrieve what he'd left: another brown nine-by-twelve-inch envelope with the same sort of lettering.

I came back in, took a deep breath, and opened it. I looked at the photograph, read the note, and looked at the photograph again. As I was sitting down on the couch with what must have been an astounded and horrified expression, Mike came into the room.

"What's wrong?" he said, sounding alarmed.

I handed him the note and the photograph.

"Holy..." He sat down next to me. "Do you know when this one was taken?"

I shook my head. Mike put his arm around me and I put my head on his shoulder. "Don't let it get to you," he said. "Someone's trying to scare you and you're letting them do it."

"How can I not?" I said. "It is scary. It's awful. It's like I'm being stalked. And this one's taken in front of my own house. I knew someone was there. I could feel it."

"Maybe we should just bag this whole thing."

"I can't do that," I said. "I have to find out who killed him."

"Beth."

I didn't answer.

"Beth, there's no reason on earth why you have to be the one to solve this murder. It's going to be solved with you or without you. You know that, don't you?"

I sat for a while in silence. "Well, I'll think about quitting," I eventually said, "but I'm not promising anything."

"That's all I ask," he said, and he gave me a kiss on the top of my head. "And I suggest you share this with Brian McHenry, immediately."

"I'm going to call him right now."

Mike planted another kiss on my forehead, gave me one of those chin-up looks, and left the room. I went into the kitchen and dialed Brian's office number. He didn't answer and the person who finally picked up the phone said he was "currently unavailable." Well, that was just great.

I made a cup of tea and tried to get some work done, but just couldn't concentrate. Ten minutes later, I tried Brian's number again. Same response. After three more futile attempts, I asked if he was actually in the building and was told that he was so I took the photo and the note, told everyone I'd be back a little later, and drove to his office on Seventh and State. When I walked in I spotted him from a distance but he didn't see me. He was leaning back in his desk chair, a charming and unmistakably seductive look on his face, while Ms. What's-Her-Name, the police-woman who'd interviewed me at Don's office the night he was killed, twirled a lock of hair with her fingers and gushed and flirted with him like a teen-ager. I looked back and forth between the two of them, both talking quietly and occasionally leaning closer to each other to whisper. She looked like a puppy in love and he looked like his tail was wagging.

My face felt hot, tears welled up, and my heart was pounding. I actually felt sick to my stomach. I was already about as upset as I could be and this was more than I could handle just then. I did my best to appear normal and sane, walked calmly toward his desk, slammed the envelope down so hard it made both of them jump (they'd been oblivious up to that point), turned, and walked out. I heard Brian call my name but I kept going.

When I got home, my phone was ringing but I let

the machine pick it up. It was Brian. He said, "Beth, please call me. It's urgent."

Urgent. Yeah, right.

I went into the library, made an absolute fool of myself banging things around, groaning and sighing a lot, and finally gave up and went to the kitchen. I drank three cups of tea hoping the urge to call him would go away, but it didn't so I got it over with.

"What's so urgent?" I barked when he picked up.

"Beth, what in the world is wrong with you? What did I do?"

Now what was I supposed to say? "You were talking to another woman and I hate you for it"? Even in my hideously agitated mood, I knew that was irrational.

"What's going on with you and Miss What's-Her-Face?" I asked in a voice I actually perceived as calm.

"Miss Whom?" he said, sounding annoyed.

"You know who I'm talking about."

"You mean the officer who was speaking to me when you came in?"

"Yes, Brian. *That* one."

"What about her?" he said.

"If there's something going on between you, that's your choice, but I just want you to be honest with me about it."

He made a sound feigning incredulity and astonishment. "What are you talking about? She's just a coworker. She's new in the department and I've been

helping her learn the ropes. You're just being paranoid, Beth. You're imagining things.''

How many times have I heard that one? I took a
few deep breaths and tried to get rid of the lump in
my throat. It wouldn't go away.

"Beth?" Brian said. "Are you there?"

I took another breath. "If you want to see someone
else," I managed in a shaky voice, "you're perfectly
entitled to. I just think it's only fair that you let me
know about it.''

"Beth, I don't want to see anyone else. There is
no one else. Trust me.''

"I don't believe you," I said, my voice sounding
teary.

He sighed. Then he sighed again. "Beth, you're out
of control. I'll talk to you about this when you've
calmed down. Now tell me about this photo.''

I didn't say anything.

"Beth, this is serious. These are deliberate, unmis-
takable threats. This is a picture of you in front of
your own house after dark and the note says *Home
Sweet Home,* so we know he knows you live there.
You're being followed and I want…''

I didn't hear the rest of what he said. I was too
busy thinking. "Brian, how could someone take a picture like that when it was completely dark? I never
even saw a flash.''

"There are cameras that take night pictures. Of
course, the average person isn't likely to own one.

Are any of your suspects photographers?'' he asked in a teasing voice.

"Not that I know of," I said, succumbing to his charm. "Are any of yours?"

"Nope. Not so far."

We talked a bit longer but then he said he had to go. I felt a little better than I had before I'd called but I was still hurting a lot. I know I was acting crazy, letting jealousy control my thoughts, but I couldn't seem to help it just then.

It was a little after noon, around our usual lunchtime, and Em, Janice, and Mike came into the kitchen all at once. "What's the matter with you?" Emily said.

"Nothing," I muttered, and looked away. My face was red, I could feel it.

We had turkey sandwiches and coleslaw. Mike and Em were arguing over some obscure point of law and Janice asked me how I was doing on the investigation.

"I got another picture and note in the mail today," I said, and I described them both.

"Oh, my gosh," Janice said. "They must be following you wherever you go."

I nodded with a sick look. But then I had a thought and my face brightened. "Hey, you know what? The timing of the pictures—assuming I get more, that is— might help me figure out who it could be."

She creased her brow.

"Well, it can't be just anybody depending on when they're taken or where they're taken. Like someone who absolutely had to be somewhere else at a certain time couldn't have taken the picture.''

''Unless they hired someone to do it,'' Janice said.

''Yeah, but I don't think they'd do that. Assuming it's Don's murderer who's sending me this stuff, it'd be too risky to hire someone else.''

''Well, that's true,'' she said.

WE FINISHED THE DAY at five-thirty. I walked up and down the stairs fifty times, took a shower, changed my clothes, had a cup of tea, and headed for the Coffee Trader on Downer to meet Miss Andrews.

The Coffee Trader used to be nothing but a little cheese-and-coffee shop when I was in high school. Now it's an airy and spacious full-service restaurant with high ceilings and expansive windows all along the Downer Avenue wall. The tables are wooden, the ceiling fans are always on when you need them, and lush green plants thrive along with the business. It's often referred to as a sort of chic-hip-yuppie-cool place to be, but even if you're *totally uncool* like I'm so often accused of being, you'd like it anyway.

I found a parking space a block and a half away, entered the restaurant, and suddenly realized I had no idea what Miss Andrews looked like. I wasn't even sure of her approximate age, though her voice sounded pretty young. I told the hostess I was waiting for someone and she pointed to a table for two at which a young woman of about twenty-five was seated.

"Is that her?" she asked.

"To tell you the truth, I have no idea. I've never met her. Did she tell you her name?"

The fifty-something hostess gave me a wry look. "Dana Andrews. Can you believe that?"

I laughed. "Well, I think she's the one I'm looking for. Thanks."

I walked toward the table and Dana A. watched as I approached, an expectant and openly friendly look on her face.

"Dana Andrews?" I said.

She stood halfway and held out her hand with a big smile. "Hi. You're Beth?"

I nodded. "Beth Hartley," I said. "I really appreciate your doing this. I need all the help I can get."

"Oh, it's no problem. I think what happened to Mr. Balstrum is just terrible, don't you?"

"Well…yeah," I said.

"So who do you think did it?" she asked, her eyes opening wide, her body leaned forward in expectation.

"I don't know yet, I haven't learned enough. I really need to know a lot more about Mr. Balstrum. Now, you were his secretary, right?"

"That's right," she said with an emphatic nod. "For five years."

"Had his caseload changed recently?"

Dana squinted and thought for a while. "Well, my workload wasn't any different. That's all I can tell you. We've always had a lot of business."

"So he got a lot of cases?"

"Oh, yeah," she said. "He was really successful. He was one of the most sought-after divorce attorneys in Milwaukee."

I'd never heard that but I supposed it could be true.

"Dana, can you think of anything that went on in the office that seemed weird to you, even if it didn't involve Mr. Balstrum directly?"

She stared off into space for a while. "Well, I always thought it was kind of weird how *Mrs*. Balstrum used to come to the office and start big screaming fights with him right in the middle of the day. Now tell me that isn't weird?"

I nodded in agreement. "Anything else? Think hard. And take your time."

Dana thought and she thought. "Wellll," she said, "there *was* something."

"What?" I said.

"It was Mr. Balstrum and Mr. Nolte. I think they were mad at each other."

"Why do you think that?"

"Because they wouldn't even talk to each other anymore."

"When did that start?" I asked, feeling pretty sure I knew the answer.

"It was at least six months before Mr. Balstrum got killed."

"Do you have any idea what it was about?"

Dana shook her head. "Nobody knew. One day Mr. Nolte just ordered Mr. Balstrum to come to his office and after that they wouldn't say one word to each other. It was pretty childish, if you ask me."

"Did you overhear anything they said?"

"No, none of us did. Or if they did, they sure weren't talking about it."

I thought about that for a moment. "What about Mr. Nolte's secretary? Do you think she could know something?"

"No, Barbara wasn't working here then. Elise Jacobs was Mr. Nolte's secretary at the time but she quit right after it happened."

"She quit?" I said. "Why did she do that?"

Dana put a perturbed look on her face. "Good question," she said. "Elise and I were pretty good friends—or at least I thought we were—but she wouldn't tell me anything. She wouldn't even talk about it. She just cleared out her desk and left right in the middle of the day and she never even called me back and I left at *least* ten messages on her answering machine."

"Would you mind giving me her number?" I asked.

Dana recited the number by rote. "Do me a favor," she said. "When you talk to her, just tell her I'm really hurt she won't even answer my calls. I thought we were better friends than that."

"I'll do that," I said. "Dana, can you think of anything else that might help me?"

"No, I really can't. You don't think Mr. Nolte did it, do you?"

"Well, let's put it this way," I said. "Everyone's a suspect to begin with, but other than that, I don't have any special reason to believe he did it."

"Good," she said with a big sigh. "I'd hate to think I was working for a murderer."

I forced a smile and handed Dana one of my cards. She agreed to call if she thought of anything new.

I went home, had a cup of decaf tea, and read for a few hours before I went to bed. I decided to give Cassandra Balstrum a call the next day. And maybe Elise Jacobs. Glen Nolte, I was saving for later.

THE NEXT DAY was Wednesday, October 28. Mrs. Gunther came in early and gave me some very bad news. Erma did indeed have cancer and it had metastasized to just about everywhere as far as they could tell. Mrs. Gunther was so calm when she told me, I guessed she must be in shock. I sat her down, made her a cup of tea, and started with simple questions, like: "How is Erma feeling? How is she taking it?"

Mrs. Gunther answered, "She's in a lot of pain," and "Quite well, considering." Then her lip quivered and she started to cry, quietly at first and then big trembling sobs. I hugged her and stroked her hair until she stopped, nearly ten minutes later.

"What happens next?" I said when I thought she was ready to talk again.

She let out a big, teary sigh. "Chemotherapy starts first thing next week if they feel she's strong enough."

I hugged her again. "No matter when it is, I want you to call me if you need me for anything at all. And I also want you to know that you have all the time off you need. As much time as you want. You don't even have to call me to tell me you're not coming."

She looked at me with tears in her eyes. I gave her a loving smile, got up, and refilled her empty teacup. When she insisted on getting to work, I spent a few minutes pulling myself together and then I called Cassandra Balstrum. I got their voice mail but I decided not to leave a message for the time being. I called David next and asked him where I might reach her.

"She's at work," he said, "but she's hard to catch. She's an interior decorator and she's usually out of the office." He gave me the number anyway.

I dialed and a woman picked up, very soft-spoken, an almost ethereal voice. Really annoying. I asked for Cassandra but she wasn't in, just as David had predicted. That time, I did leave a message.

I went into the library, gave Em, Janice, and Mike the news about Erma, and we talked about that for a while. Janice cried a little and Mike looked as if he might. Emily's expression barely changed. Sometimes I really wonder about Emily—whether she ever feels anything for anyone. Or maybe it's just that Erma and Mrs. Gunther aren't among the deserving chosen few.

I got to work then on one of David's projects (they were actually rather difficult), all the while watching the clock, waiting for the postman.

At eleven-twelve, I heard the box open and shut, then his retreating footsteps. I sat right where I was for several minutes. Janice looked at me and frowned.

"What's the matter?" she said.

"The mail."

She got up, took hold of my arm, and escorted me to the door. "Do you want me to open it for you?" she asked when I removed it from the mailbox.

My hands were shaking so badly I could barely hold on to it. I felt like I was overreacting but I couldn't stop myself.

"Yes," I said, and handed her the envelope.

Janice removed the contents with a mixture of fear and anticipation showing on her face. She only frowned when she looked at the photograph but when she saw the note, she inhaled sharply and held her breath. She handed me the picture, first.

"I don't recognize this place," she said.

I did. It was Mr. and Mrs. Balstrum's house. Mike and I had been there to see Mrs. Balstrum, though the picture was taken at such an angle that I was in it and Mike was not.

Then she showed me the note. I flinched and walked back to the library with Janice behind me.

"You got another one, didn't you?" Mike said when he saw my face.

I handed it to him. "Isn't this the Balstrum place?" he asked.

I nodded.

"But I was with you. Why aren't I in the picture?"

I gave him what I'm sure was a rather ill look and handed him the note. He read it and his face blanched. *MIsSinG aNotHer FRIenD?* it said.

Mike sat down and stared at his feet. Then suddenly he looked up. "When did you say the first picture was taken?"

"Hold on a minute." I took the Don file from my desk and paged through my notes. "Wednesday, October twenty-first."

"And what about the second one?"

"That was the one taken in front of my house. I'm not sure. But I think it could've been the night I thought someone was watching me." I thought for a moment and searched for the date. "That would've been Friday, the twenty-third."

"And when did we go to see Mrs. Balstrum?"

I looked through the notes again. "Thursday, October twenty-second."

"They're out of order," Mike said.

"But why should that matter?" I asked.

"Maybe he has a backlog and he's holding them until he feels like sending them."

"But why would he do that?"

"I don't know. Maybe he thinks the effect will be stronger that way."

"Then maybe he's no longer following you," Janice said, her voice sounding hopeful.

"I wouldn't count on that," I said. "If this guy is trying to scare me—and I know he is—he'll make sure I know he's still following me."

Oh, how right I was.

At one-thirty, Cassandra returned my call, identified herself, and asked what I wanted, all very coolly. I told her who I was, reminded her that we'd met briefly at the viewing, and asked if I might speak with her sometime about Don.

There was a long pause. "Why?" she asked.

"I need to talk to as many people as I can who knew Don and had some familiarity with his life."

"We rarely saw each other."

"Nevertheless, I'm sure you must know more about him than someone who never met him." (That made perfect sense to me when I said it, but unlike my writing, I can't go back and edit my conversations.)

"I can hardly debate that," she said with obvious sarcasm.

"Then you'll agree to see me?" I said.

"I didn't say that."

"Please, Mrs. Balstrum, I could really use your help. I promise not to take too much time and it would be entirely at your convenience. You name the time and place." When she didn't respond, I said, "Please," again.

"Oh, very well," she said. "I'll see you in my home. Let us say tomorrow night, eight o'clock?"

"That would be fine," I said. "Thank you so much. I really appreciate this, Mrs. Balstrum."

"I'll see you tomorrow night then," she said with

a little more warmth. "And call me Cassandra. I detest being called Mrs. Balstrum."

I grinned as I hung up. For some reason, I was particularly anxious to talk with her, though I wished she'd chosen a time when David was less likely to be there.

I worked very hard for the rest of the day and continued for at least another hour and a half after everyone had left. By then, I was starving so I stopped to have something to eat and discovered I was out of food (I mean totally out of food or at least anything I would've considered eating). I hate grocery shopping but I had to do it so I decided to go to Sendik's.

It was almost totally dark, the moon nothing but a little sliver. I pulled my jacket collar up to block out the cold wind and walked toward my car.

But something didn't feel right. Again.

EIGHT

I LOOKED AROUND, scanning my yard and the perimeter of my house, but I couldn't see very well. My neighbor's ground lights were on this time, but they barely reach my yard so my vision was still very limited. Once more, I had the sense that someone was there, hiding in the darkness. I tried to act as calm as possible as I got in my car, locked the doors, and pulled out of the driveway. On the drive there, I told myself over and over that I couldn't allow this to control my life. I wasn't going to let it get to me.

Forty minutes later, I was back and I felt it again. I collected my groceries, walked very deliberately to the door, but then I fumbled with the lock. I couldn't get the key in while holding three bags of groceries. I put the groceries down, tried again, and dropped my keys. As I searched for them, I heard all sorts of sounds, the volume magnified by my fearful mind. Leaves rustling, wind moving through the trees, the screech of a tire. Something moved in a bush and I screamed. After what seemed like hours, I spotted my keys in one of the bags, managed to unlock the door, and literally threw everything inside.

I didn't sleep well at all that night. Nor the night after that.

THURSDAY, OCTOBER 29. My mother called, first thing.

"I thought you were coming over last Friday. What happened to you?"

I smiled. It'd taken her almost a week to remember. "I'm sorry, Mom, I just forgot. I had to have dinner with someone and it was late by the time we were finished so I just went home to bed."

"Who'd you have dinner with?" she asked in her mother-checking-up-on-her-child voice, with an entirely ineffective attempt to sound perfectly innocent.

"A friend, Mom. Actually, it was Don Balstrum's twin brother, the guy I told you about."

No response.

"What's wrong, Mom?" I was already irritated and my voice showed it. I knew exactly what she was thinking.

"I wish you'd stay out of police business, Elizabeth. I know you always wanted to be a spy when you were a child but you're grown up now. Or maybe you're not."

I clenched my teeth and remained silent.

"I'll never forget the time you came to me and your father and said you'd decided to join the FBI. You were already in high school, for heaven's sake. And you were still looking for secret passageways in the house. For the life of me, I don't know what comes over you sometimes."

I sighed.

"And then there was the time Mr. and Mrs. Dayton

came over and complained because they'd caught you standing under their kitchen window writing down everything they said and did in that notebook of yours. You'd even recorded the times. Do you remember that?''

"Yes, Mom, I remember. I was just a little kid. They never said anything the least bit interesting anyway so what difference did it make? *And,*" I added before she had a chance to respond, "if they had said anything like I'd expected them to say, then everyone, including you, would have been very grateful to me because I would've solved a murder."

She let out an exasperated groan. "Beth, you're not a child anymore but for some reason I've never been able to fathom, you still live in a fantasy world. You always have, from the day you were born."

I was getting really tired of the whole conversation by that time. "Mom, I don't want to talk about it anymore. This isn't a fantasy. It's a real murder of a real person whom I knew and liked very much. Now just leave me alone."

She made a last and futile attempt. "Brian won't like you interfering, you know. You're going to lose him and you're not getting any younger."

"Any younger for *what*, Mom?"

"For marriage, young lady. You know darn well what I'm talking about. Do you want to live alone for the rest of your life?"

I laughed. "How about this, Mom? Do *you* want to have to tell all our friends and relatives that your oldest daughter is getting married again? For the *third time?*"

"Well," she said after a few moments of silence. "When are we going to see you with this busy schedule of yours?"

"How about Sunday morning? I'd say Saturday but it's Halloween and I want to be here for trick-or-treat."

"Fine," she said tersely. "We'll see you on Sunday."

I tried Elise Jacobs (Glen Nolte's former secretary) after that, assuming I'd get an answering machine, and I did. I thought of leaving a message but decided against it. I wanted to catch her offguard the first time I talked to her.

I was seeing Cassandra at her house at eight that evening and I wanted to do the best I could to get one of David's projects done before the end of the day so I could drop it off at his office. I brought a chicken salad sandwich into the library at lunch time and was just about to get back to work when I remembered I hadn't retrieved my mail. I wasted five minutes trying to decide if I even wanted to look at it and finally convinced myself that I needed to know, whether I liked it or not. I went to the door, opened the box, and grinned. There was nothing there but regular, ordinary mail. A very good sign—unless he planned on a personal delivery.

I went back to the library, immersed myself in my work, and finished David's brief by a quarter to four, just as I had hoped. Janice had been typing as I worked so it took only ten minutes more to have the completed product. She made a copy for our files while I had a quick cup of tea, and then I headed for David's office without even bothering to call. As I was leaving, I asked Mike if he'd like to come with me that night to see Cassandra. He said he would.

WHEN I ARRIVED AT David's office, he was in with a client so I told the receptionist not to bother him until he was through. As I leafed through a magazine in the lobby, a middle-aged man wearing a wrinkled pin-striped suit without the jacket, a rumpled shirt and tie, and colorfully striped suspenders that stretched tautly over his large paunch, walked through and asked the receptionist if there had been any messages for him.

"Just one, Mr. Bailey," she said politely and handed him a pink slip of paper.

I hesitated just a moment and got up and followed him. "Mr. Bailey?" I said in a timid voice.

He turned around, looked at me and smiled broadly. "Yes, I'm Clem Bailey. How can I be of service to you?"

"Can we talk privately?" I asked.

He looked slightly perplexed but told the receptionist to hold his calls. "Right this way," he said with a look bordering on flirtation. I had the impression he hadn't used it in a while.

Since I hadn't planned on a Clem Bailey interview, I'd never given any thought to what I wanted to ask him. I was still sort of frantically trying to come up with something when he showed me to his office and offered me a seat. He sat behind his desk, leaned forward (a lot), and grinned. I decided right then that it wouldn't matter what I asked. He was too involved in his own thoughts to care.

I leaned forward, too, and he leaned even more, bumping his substantial stomach on the edge of the desk. "Mr. Bailey," I began.

"Clem, please." Big smile, then a starry-eyed, ruminative look.

"Clem," I said sweetly, "you must know David pretty well."

No change in expression.

"I knew Don from law school," I said, "but I only met David after Don died."

Clem shifted in his seat and sat back a little. "I've known Dave quite a few years," he said. "He was opposing counsel on a tough-as-nails products liability case. I'd been second-chairing trials for three years and it was the first one I tried myself. Dave was a tad bit more seasoned than I," he said with a wry smile, "and I admired him greatly. He's a top-notch lawyer. One of the best I've seen."

I smiled. "So I've heard," I said. "How about Don? Did you know him?"

Clem leaned his head to one side. "I'd met him," he said, emphasizing the word "met," "but I never really got to know him. He came by the office pretty regularly but it was usually no more than a nod and a 'hello' between us."

"I'm surprised they never practiced together," I said as if I'd thought of it for the first time.

Clem frowned slightly and cleared his throat. "Dave's taking Don's death terribly hard," he said after a few moments. "I wish I could do something, but..." He opened both palms to me.

"I know. It's really hard to know what to say or do. Has he talked about it much?"

Clem sighed. "Not in so many words. I didn't see him for a few days after it happened. I was out of town at the time and when I returned, the funeral had already been held. I called over at the house but I couldn't reach him. I couldn't bring myself to leave a message. What do you say?"

I gave him a nod and a comprehending half-smile. "When did you finally see him or talk to him?"

Clem put on a bit of a frown. "I think it was the next time I was in the office. He was here, too. Working. I must say I was surprised."

"You were surprised to see him working?"

"Yes," Clem said. "I don't know that I could have managed so soon under the circumstances."

"But he wasn't acting as if nothing had happened, was he?"

Clem looked skyward and shook his head. "No, I should say not. I've never seen him like this. He's disoriented. Really quite shaken up."

I nodded. "Yes, he seems very disturbed by the whole thing. Who wouldn't be?"

"Exactly," Clem said.

"Has he given you any indication that he suspects anyone?"

Clem frowned and gave me a surprised look. "Oh, no," he said. "I'm certain he has no idea. In truth, that may contribute to the intensity of his reaction."

"How do you mean?"

"Why, he's so utterly baffled, almost disbelieving."

"I suppose he just hasn't accepted it yet. That can take an awful long time with some people."

Clem acquired a far away look. "Yes," he said in a distracted voice. "It can." Then he looked back at me. "My wife," he said quietly. "Her mother died, very suddenly. It's been ten years now but when it happened she was in shock. It took her nearly two years to recover to the point where she was functioning at the level she had been before it happened. I was afraid she'd never be the same."

"But she's all right, now?"

"Yes," he said, smiling. "Thank you for asking."

I smiled, too, and stood to leave. "Well, I really shouldn't take anymore of your time. I appreciate your talking to me and I'm glad I had a chance to meet you."

Clem came around to the front of the desk and put his arm around my shoulder as he walked me out.

"It was my pleasure," he said. As we left Clem's

office, David appeared from his. When he saw us, he winced, very briefly, and then put a big smile on his face.

"Beth," he said. "I wasn't expecting you." He gestured toward his office. "Make yourself at home, I'll be with you in a minute."

I did as he suggested and watched David and Clem walk toward the outer lobby, their heads bent toward each other in muffled conversation.

When David returned, he gave me a brief smile and sat at his desk. "So, what's up?"

"I finished the Faulkner brief and I'm giving you the first-class treatment I award only my favorite customers: personal delivery." I grinned and he grinned back, though his was a little strained.

David held out his hand and I passed the file across the desk. He took as long as he needed to review what I had done, put everything back in the file, placed it on his desk, and looked at me.

"This is excellent work," he said. "Really superb. I'm quite impressed."

"Thank you," I said with a self-conscious smile. "I'll have the Dombrowski thing done probably by Tuesday, maybe Wednesday at the latest."

He arched his brows. "You work fast," he said.

"I've been doing it for a long time. It becomes second nature after a while."

He looked at me askance. Then he smiled, almost to himself, leaned back in his chair, and said, "How's the investigation going?"

I almost told him about the pictures but decided against it. "All right," I said. "I still have no idea who did it but at least I'm getting through my list of interviewees. I'm seeing Cassandra tonight, by the way, at your house."

David looked a bit surprised but not particularly disturbed.

We made a little small talk and then he walked me out. "By the way, what were you talking to Clem about?" he asked.

"Don," I said with a shrug.

"Did he know anything?"

"Nothing I hadn't already learned," I said.

David nodded and said good-bye.

It was nearly five-thirty by then, dark and extremely windy. A relentless rain was falling, predictably unpredicted by our weather bureau, and it was a cold, miserable rain mixed with sleet—a little unusual this early in the season but certainly not unheard of. By the time I reached my car, my hair and clothing were soaked, my face stung from the ice, and I couldn't stop shivering.

I put the car away when I got home though I'd have to take it out again when I went to see Cassandra. I remembered then that I'd forgotten to mention to David that Mike would be coming along.

Mike, Em, and Janice had gone home by then so I had the place all to myself. The rain and ice were pelting my windows, coming in spurts and dashes. I made myself a cup of tea, sat down at the kitchen table, and cradled the cup in my hands as I took slow sips and listened to the storm. The tea warmed me up and the rain had a calming effect, despite its force. Rain tapping on my roof and windowpanes is one of my very favorite sounds.

I made beef stew and hot biscuits for dinner and paged through my Don file while I waited for it to cook. I added notes about my conversations with Clem and David and made a list of the people I thought I'd like to talk with next: Cassandra, of course, Glen, and Elise. And maybe Amy, again.

By the time I'd finished my dinner, changed my clothes, and fixed my hair, Mike had arrived and we were off. The rain was coming down a bit harder now and there was more ice than water. The roads were horrendously slippery and I almost turned back, but I'd seen two salt trucks already so I decided to keep going. We didn't have far to go anyway, and most of my travel was on a main road (Lincoln Memorial Drive). I crept along at twenty-five miles per hour and, thankfully, so did everyone else.

"Cassandra," Mike said in a breathy voice. "Does she look like a Cassandra?"

"I don't know?" I said with a laugh. "I've never even known anyone named Cassandra before. You'll have to decide that for yourself."

He had a funny little smile on his face. I rolled my eyes and laughed again but he didn't notice. He was lost in thoughts I didn't even want to be let in on.

When we arrived, I parked in the ice-free circular

drive and we walked to the doorway on some very sizable chunks of salt.

David answered the door, said hello, and stared at Mike. "Cassandra's expecting you," he said to me, his eyes still on Mike.

Mike held out his hand. "Mike Shepard," he said. "I'm assisting Beth in her investigation."

"David Balstrum," David said, and shook Mike's hand. "I saw you at the viewing."

"I went to law school with Don," Mike said.

A faint smile crept onto David's face. "Did you know him well?"

"Not very," Mike said. "We studied together after class sometimes but we didn't really hang out together outside of school."

"What did you think of him?" David asked.

Mike hesitated and creased his brow. "I liked him," he said in an odd voice. "I liked him a lot."

When David smiled and started walking away, Mike shot me a quizzical look and I shrugged in response.

"Cassandra's in the parlor," David was saying. He showed us the way, announced our arrival, and ceremoniously closed the doors. Cassandra gave me a prolonged look of assessment, then a cool smile. She sort of sucked in her cheeks when she looked at Mike.

"You didn't tell me there would be three of us," she said. "Sit down," she added, without waiting for me to respond. "Would you care for coffee?"

A silver setup was already there so I said, "Yes, with cream, please." Mike said, "No, thank you."

Cassandra poured, added cream, and handed me a cup without a word. She picked up her own cup and gave me another cool inspection. I found it strange since we'd met before. She had an odd but fascinating look about her. She wasn't actually beautiful or even pretty but she seemed to exude so much confidence in her appearance that I almost felt I must be mistaken. She was very tall—at least five-nine—and slender, with long shapely legs. She kept crossing and uncrossing them, adjusting the skirt of her dress (which was calf-length with a slit a little past the knee, on the right side). Her eyes were a smoky olive green, very deepset and large. She had long auburn hair, finely lined, almost transparently pale skin, a sharp, pointed nose, and thin lips painted a light shade of rust. I realized I'd been staring at her and I looked over at Mike. He was alternately watching her legs and gazing at her face with an expression of either awe or intimidation. I wasn't sure which.

I cleared my throat and said, "I know this is an imposition, but I'm trying to talk with anyone who knew Don well enough to notice any change in his behavior over the last few months."

Cassandra's put-out look was barely perceptible, which made it all the more annoying. "I didn't know Don well," she said, almost without inflection.

"When did you meet David?" I asked.

"Twenty-five years ago." The put-out expression became less obscured.

"How long was it before you met Don?"

She huffed ever so slightly. "I met him shortly after I met David. What possible difference does it make?"

"I'm just trying to find out how long you've known Don," I said.

All I got in response to that was a cool, detached silence.

I sighed. "So they were in their early twenties when you met them?"

"Yes."

"Which one did you like better?" Mike asked, and I burst out laughing. Even Cassandra couldn't hold back an amused smile though she was trying pretty hard. Then she actually laughed as she looked at Mike's face.

"I think I liked David the best," she said with a teasing expression. "He is the one I married."

Mike grinned. "Sorry," he said. "I don't know why I said that." Then he frowned and said, "Why did you like him best?"

I rolled my eyes. Cassandra saw me and matched my expression.

"He was more my type," she said. "They were two very different people. Identical twins don't necessarily have identical personalities. You can take my word on that."

Mike smiled and looked as if he were waiting for more. It worked.

"When I met David, he was overflowing with ambition and pride. He knew where he was going and how to do it. I admired him. I never had any such impression of Don. He was lazy and immature. Nothing like David," she added with a dismissive gesture.

"How is David taking Don's death, in your opinion?" I asked.

She frowned a bit. "That's hard to answer," she said. "I'd certainly say he's not himself since the murder, but one would expect that." Then she sighed and paused a few moments. "I don't know quite how to put this, but he seems more shaken by Don's death than I would have expected. I know that sounds harsh, but David's never been an emotional person. Of course, murder is a bit more than we ordinarily expect out of life, isn't it?"

I nodded. I was about to say something when Mike intervened. "Have you ever had the impression that David envied Don?" he asked.

Cassandra almost sneered. "Of course not," she said. "Why would David be envious of Don? Certainly, it was the other way around."

"Are you saying David had a low opinion of Don?"

"Nobody thought much of Don," she said. "What was there to admire?"

That really irritated me. "He was a nice person," I said. "And he was very successful as an attorney.

His practice did extremely well and he was highly respected as a divorce lawyer."

"Sorry," Cassandra said with an amused little smile. "I didn't realize you were so close." Mike looked at me and watched my face. I glared at him and looked back at Cassandra. "We weren't close," I said. "But we were friends, not particularly close friends, but friends just the same, and I don't think you give him enough credit for who he was."

Cassandra drew in her cheeks and looked down for a few moments. "Perhaps you're right," she said as she looked up again. "I'm sorry I was so insensitive."

I gave her a forgiving smile (a little one, but it was still forgiving). "That's all right," I said. "It's hard to change your impression of someone once it's formed. Everything consistent with it just reinforces your original assessment and anything inconsistent just gets ignored or reinterpreted."

Mike looked at me like I was nuts and Cassandra simply frowned. I ignored them both.

"Did you see much of Don?" I asked.

Cassandra shook her head. "Not often," she said. "I know the two of them had lunch on occasion but Don was seldom at the house."

"Had David mentioned anything about Don being in any kind of trouble?"

Cassandra considered the question for a while. "No," she finally said, "but I did overhear them on the phone several times and I had the impression they were talking about some sort of problem Don was having. The first time it happened, David's voice was raised, which is uncommon for him, and it caught my attention. When he was through with the call, I asked him about it. He told me he'd been talking to Don and that it was something personal. The next few times, I just said, 'Don again?', and he nodded.''

"How many times did this happen?"

"Four or five, I think."

"When was the first time?" I asked.

Cassandra frowned and thought for a bit. "It would have to be nearly six months ago. Maybe a little less."

"Did you hear any of what David said?"

"Yes," she said slowly, "but I couldn't hear Don so I was never able to make much sense of it. David was responding to what Don was saying, for the most part, trying to calm him down about something, but I don't know what it was."

"Can you remember anything specific that he said?"

She sighed and put on a look of deep concentration. "Well, the first time, he said something like, 'You know what to do' or 'You know what you need to do'—something of that nature."

"Anything else?"

"I don't know, it's so hard to recall." Then she paused. "Wait a moment, I do remember something. Once—I think it was the last conversation I overheard—David had gotten quite angry and I heard him say, 'I can't bail you out of this one. You're on your own this time.'"

"Do you remember when that conversation took place?" Mike asked.

"It couldn't have been more than a few weeks before the murder."

"Maybe that's one of the reasons David seems so disturbed by his death," I said. "Maybe the last time he talked to him, they'd been fighting."

Cassandra looked stunned. "Oh, my, you may be right," she said in a low voice. She was quiet for a few moments and then she gave me a penetrating look. "Why aren't you asking David these questions instead of me?"

"I intend to," I said. "To be honest with you, it was something I hadn't thought of until now. What I really wanted to ask you about is Don's father."

She frowned and waited for me to continue.

"Has David ever mentioned anything to you about his father's restaurant business?"

She was about to speak but I interrupted her. "What I'm really interested in knowing is whether he suspected that something illegal was going on and that Don might be involved."

Cassandra took a deep breath and blew it out. "Oh, boy," she said. "I think we ought to include David in this discussion." She stood and walked toward the door.

"Wait," I said. "Please, I'd really prefer to talk with you separately. I can assure you I'll ask David the same questions but I don't want you to be influenced by each other when you answer.''

Her expression betrayed a certain amount of annoyance, but she agreed. When I repeated the question, she looked at Mike and back at me.

''When Don was still in law school,'' she began, ''he came to David bragging that Art had hired him to give him legal advice from time to time. David was incensed. He'd been practicing law for over five years and Don was just a student but Art had never once approached David for advice. Then, sometime later, David told me he'd suspected for a long time that Art was engaged in some sort of illegal activity involving the restaurants and he was quite sure that Don must not only know about it but that he might be involved himself because he spent so much time over there. So David asked him about it—Don, that is—but he insisted that nothing was going on and that everything Art was doing was on the up and up.''

''Did David believe him?'' I said.

''No, of course not, but what could he do? He wasn't going to approach Art and Don was just impenetrable, so he let the matter drop.''

''But it bothered him a lot,'' I said.

''Yes, of course it bothered him.''

''Did David have any specific ideas about what the illegal activity might be?''

Cassandra wrinkled her nose. ''He thinks it might be income tax evasion but on a very large scale. He said something about money-laundering but I'm not sure what he meant.''

Mike was nodding and smiling to himself and I stared at him with a look of amazement. ''You suspected that, too?'' I asked him.

''It crossed my mind,'' he said.

''What does this mean in relation to Don's death?'' Cassandra said with a concern I hadn't detected before.

''Probably nothing,'' I said, hoping to ease her anxiety. ''It just gives us a fuller picture of Don's life before he died.''

She nodded and looked lost in thought so I signaled to Mike that I wanted to leave. Mike stood up and offered Cassandra his hand. ''Thank you so much for your time, Mrs. Balstrum. We won't keep you any longer.''

She gave him an absentminded smile and said, ''You're welcome.''

When we got in the car, Mike was unusually quiet. I looked over at him but he didn't turn his head toward me. ''So what do you think?'' I said in a cautious voice.

He sighed and then shrugged, pulling his head into his jacket like a big turtle. ''I don't know. What do you think?''

I frowned. ''Well, obviously, Don was in some kind of big trouble, David knew all about it and refused to help him, and it could be related to either the embezzlement or some shady business—whether it's tax evasion or something else—at Balstrum's restaurants.''

Mike didn't say a word.

"Is something bothering you?" I said.

No answer.

"Mike, what's wrong?"

He shrugged again, sighed loudly, and looked out the side window. Then he sighed again.

Now I was getting impatient. "Mike, what's the matter? What's bothering you?"

I could barely hear him, he answered so softly. "Don called me a couple of weeks before he died," he said.

"Don called you?" I said. "Why didn't you tell me that? What did he say?"

"He left a message on my machine. He asked me to call him but when I did, he wasn't there, so I left him a message and I never called again. I figured he'd call me back."

"Why didn't you mention this before?"

"I don't know," Mike said. "I was worried. I was afraid I'd be considered a suspect because of it. I figured nobody would know if I kept my mouth shut so I did. I kept my mouth shut. It's as simple as that." He shoved his hands in his pockets and retreated even farther into his turtle shell.

"So why are you telling me now?" I said gently.

No response.

"Mike, you can't feel guilty because you didn't call him back again. It was perfectly logical and normal for you to assume he'd make the next call. You left him a message and you called him right away. That's all anyone would have done. It was a perfectly normal, legitimate response.''

He remained speechless but he pulled his head out a little.

"I know what you're thinking," I said. "You think he wanted to ask you for help and maybe you could've done something and now you're feeling guilty about it, right?''

His head came out a little farther and he shifted in his seat.

I reached over and touched his arm. "You couldn't have known that," I said. "And for all you know, that wasn't even what he wanted. Did he sound upset on the message?''

Mike shrugged. "A little."

"Well, how did he sound? Try to remember, exactly. And try to remember what he said."

Mike sighed and thought for a while. "He said, 'Mike, this is Don Balstrum. Please give me a call at my office.' And then he gave me the number. He said if I called after some time—I forget what it was—I should call him at home and he gave me that number, too.''

"Where did you end up calling him?"

"I called him at home because it was past the time he'd given me for the office by the time I got the message.''

"But nobody answered."

"Right, so I left a message. What else could I do?"

"Nothing," I said with emphasis. "There was nothing else you could've done and there was nothing else you should've done. Believe me, no one would've expected anymore of you."

He looked over and gave me a weak smile.

"How did his voice sound?" I asked.

"Normal, maybe a little urgent, but not worried. More like he was just in a hurry." He shook his head. "I don't know. It's hard to say. It didn't seem significant at the time."

"When was the last time you had talked to him?"

"That's the weird part," Mike said. "I hadn't talked to him once since we graduated from law school."

I thought about that for a few moments. "I wonder if he called anyone else," I said. "Maybe he was trying everyone he knew who might be willing to help him. Maybe he never got back to you because he got someone else."

Mike's eyebrows shot up. "Hey, you might be right," he said. "We could go through the Lawyers' Index."

"What for?" I said.

He gave me one of his Get-with-it looks. "So we can call around and find out if he talked to anybody else."

I said, "Good thinking, Sherlock," and he grinned like a little kid.

It was almost ten when we reached my house so

we decided to postpone the flurry of phone calls until the next day, maybe even the weekend.

"I'll see you tomorrow," Mike said when I dropped him at his car.

I watched him drive away, put my own car in the garage, and was almost at my door, lost in reflection, when someone's hands reached out and grabbed me by the shoulders.

NINE

I SCREAMED and two strong arms turned me around.

"Brian, you scared me half to death. What's the matter with you?" Most of what I said came out in a screech.

"I'm sorry," he said, looking as flustered as he sounded. "I just assumed you heard me. Where were you anyway?"

I stiffened a little. "Mike Shepard and I went to see Cassandra Balstrum."

Brian sighed, put his arm around my shoulder, and gave me a hug. "I'm sorry," he said again. "Can we go inside?"

"Sure," I said, feeling as insecure and worried as I could be. I was so glad to see him but I wasn't sure why he was there. I hadn't talked to him since we'd had our big argument over Ms. What's-Her-Name, so I was afraid it might be a good-bye visit.

I took his coat, hung it in the closet along with mine, and gave him a self-conscious smile. "Do you want some hot chocolate or something?"

His smile was nice and warm but sort of sad at the same time. "Sure. Hot chocolate would be good. It's really nasty out there tonight."

"Yeah," I agreed, feeling more anxious by the moment.

Brian followed me into the kitchen and stared out my window while I made him his cocoa. When it was ready, I placed the mug on the table and sat down. He turned around and took a chair directly across from me, picked up the cup, looked about to say something, and stopped himself. I didn't know what to say, either, so neither of us said a word. I wanted so badly to act nonchalant but I was already faltering, looking glum, trying to sneak peeks at his face when I thought he wasn't looking (which he always was). After being caught three times, I just kept my eyes on his and didn't try to hide the sadness I was feeling. I'd worked so hard to convince myself I didn't care and I'd done pretty well so long as he wasn't there, but seeing him again and being so close to him was bringing back every fond, loving, poignant, hurtful emotion I'd ever felt.

"Beth," Brian said in a nearwhisper. "We really need to talk."

My worst fears had come true, I just knew it.

He swallowed hard and cleared his throat. "I don't know where this relationship of ours is going," he said. I opened my mouth to say something but he interrupted me. "Just let me get this off my chest."

I breathed in and out, brushed away a tear, and waited.

"Beth, you're getting out of control," he said. "It's like you're paranoid I'm going to leave you or cheat on you and you get so crazy about it you can't even see what's going on in front of you.''

Tears were streaming down my face by this time but I just let them go. Brian had his eyes on his hands as he spoke so he didn't notice, anyway.

''I am not seeing anyone else and I haven't seen anyone else since I've been with you.'' He spread his hands on the table. ''Beth, you are the only woman I want to be with right now. I've told you that so many times but it's as if you never hear what I'm saying. You have some voice in your head telling you I'm cheating on you that's so loud you can't hear anything else.''

He looked up. ''I am not cheating on you. I am not going to cheat on you. I'm not even thinking about cheating on you. Whatever you think you saw between Roberta Roberson and me, you misunderstood. If you think I was flirting with her you were mistaken. Or if I was I didn't mean to.''

I opened my mouth and stared at him.

''What I mean is, if I got a little friendly I didn't mean anything by it. It's just the way I interact with women. It doesn't mean I'm coming on to them.'' He gave me a look that pleaded for me to understand. I was trying as hard as I could. I attempted a smile and came pretty close. His eyes softened and he reached for my hand.

''Honey, I don't want to lose you,'' he said, ''but please, you have to help me on this. You have to learn to trust me. I don't know what else I can do. I know your first husband cheated on you but I'm not him. I'm me and I would never do that to you. Can't you get that through your head?''

''I'm trying,'' I said. ''I'm sorry, I know I do that but I just can't help it. I'm just so afraid of being rejected that I see it happening even before it does.''

He smiled in his gentle, kind way. ''I know, honey, but the trouble is you end up making it happen when things would have been just fine if you'd let them alone.''

''Did I make it happen with you?''

''No, baby,'' he said softly. ''I'm still here and I'm not going to leave you.''

When I burst into tears his face crumpled into a confusion of tenderness and exasperation. ''That was supposed to make you feel good,'' he said.

''It does,'' I said. ''I'm crying because I'm happy. I'm just emotional, that's all.''

He gave me a crooked smile. ''I'm not going to pretend to know what you mean by that. I suppose it's just one of those woman things, huh?''

I laughed as the last few tears ran down my face.

THE NEXT DAY was Friday, October 30. I woke up early and started on another of David's projects, though I hadn't completely finished the one I was working on. They were similar in a number of ways, involving some identical legal issues, and I thought it might be more efficient to overlap them a bit. It turned out I was right. I was actually able to use an entire section from one memo for the other, with only a few, very minor changes.

By the time I'd finished that section, Mrs. Gunther, Janice, Mike, and Emily had all shown up. I went to the kitchen for tea and a chance to check in with Mrs. Gunther. She was standing at the window, watching a squirrel bury an acorn, with a vacant expression on her face. She still had her coat on and her purse was dangling from her hand.

"Mrs. Gunther?" I said.

She lifted and lowered her shoulders and slowly turned around. She was so pale it startled me.

"Oh, my gosh," I said. "What's happened? Are you all right?"

She tried to tell me something but all she could say was, "Erma..." She was beginning to sway on her feet so I went to her and gently lowered her to a chair. She sat very still for what seemed a very long time. Then she looked me straight in the eye, tears brimming in hers.

"Erma died last night," she said. Her voice was a mere whisper but her face was an anguished scream.

Mrs. Gunther kept her eyes on me and I stood silent, staring at her and crying. It had happened so fast. It was too soon. She was supposed to get better. The chemotherapy was going to cure her and everything would be all right. I wanted to go back a few hours and have the scene replayed. Couldn't we just do it over again another way? Just change the ending. It would be so easy.

Minutes went by and I hadn't said a word nor made any move to comfort her. I finally sat down, put my arms around her, and sobbed on her shoulder as if I were the one in need of comfort. She put her arms around me and sobbed all over my hair.

Our crying apparently had been audible enough to reach the library because Janice and Mike appeared in the doorway, and Emily a minute later. I gave Janice and Mike a look that both instinctively understood. They came over and sat down, held Mrs. Gunther's hands, and alternately kissed her and hugged her. I looked at Emily and she mouthed, "What happened?"

"Erma died," I mouthed back.

"What?" she mouthed back.

I closed my eyes as they teared in exasperation, got up, and pulled Emily into the next room. "Mrs. Gunther's sister died last night," I whispered, "and she didn't expect it to happen so soon."

Emily stared at me for a long time with her lips slightly parted, then looked toward the kitchen. A moment later, she started to cry. I reached out a hand to touch her shoulder but I drew it back. As you may already know, Emily is something of an enigma to me. She's closed up. The emotions and feelings have to be there, I keep telling myself, but they're so well protected, they rarely surface. When they do, I think they frighten her and they unnerve me. I'm never quite sure what she's going to do to push them back, or even worse, what might happen if she isn't able to.

"Emily," I whispered, "come in the library and sit down." She looked at me and once more toward the kitchen, then followed me.

When we reached the library, I closed the doors and pulled up a chair after she sat at her desk. She was looking down, staring at her hands, picking at her fingernails. This was very hard for me. With Emily—or anyone like her, for that matter—it's difficult not only to know how to offer comfort but whether to offer it at all. I'm afraid it might only make things worse by implicitly validating the emotions she's trying so hard to repress. Not that that isn't a good idea. It just might be the wrong time. After a moment's consideration, though, I decided this was a rare opportunity I shouldn't pass by.

"Erma was her only living relative," I said, as I carefully watched Emily's face. "She loved her very much and they were very close, all their lives."

Tears fell onto Emily's hands as she continued to look down at them.

"You care about Mrs. Gunther more than you realized, don't you?" I said gently.

She let out a sob and nodded.

"It would probably do both of you a great deal of good if you let her know that," I said, "just by telling her you're sorry about Erma or even by hugging her if you feel you can't say anything. I know her well enough to know she'd get the message from even the smallest gesture.''

Emily shuddered as she released a gush of tears.

"I know you've never made friends with her but she's a very understanding person. She knows you're not the demonstrative type. She doesn't hold that against you. She doesn't expect you to be someone you aren't.''

Emily looked up and into my eyes as if she were searching for reassurance.

"I really mean that," I said. "I've known her all my life. She's often said to me that people are who they are and you can't expect them to be someone they're not. She also says there's good in everyone, even if you can't see it. It might be hidden deep inside but it's there, somewhere, waiting to be let out. The world would be an awfully boring place, you know, if we were all the same.''

Emily laughed and sobbed at the same time. Just then, we heard someone coming, so she quickly wiped her face, turned around, and bent over her desk, pretending to work. I went over to mine and did the same. Mike and Janice came in, gave me sad looks, and sat down. A few minutes later, Emily quietly got up and left the room. As she was closing the doors behind her, she gave me the warmest and most humble smile I'd ever seen on her beautiful face.

About half an hour later, Emily returned, sat down without a glance or a word, and went back to work. She didn't look upset. In fact she looked sort of calm.

Almost serene. Several minutes later, Mrs. Gunther tapped on the door frame and I went out to meet her.

"If it's all right with you, honey, I'm going to go now," she said. "I just stopped by to tell you the news."

I nodded and tried to smile. We walked to the living room. "The wake's tomorrow night, seven p.m. at Wilkerson," she said in a monotone.

"Where's that?" I asked.

"On West Center, thirty-four-hundred block." She gave me a plaintive look. "You will be there, won't you?"

"My gosh," I said. "Of course, I will. Of course I'll be there. And please, if there's anything I can do, please, please let me know. You're more than just one of my dearest friends, you know. You're a part of my family."

Her face crumpled and she held me close. "You're the only family I have now, Bethy. I love you, honey. I always have." Then she opened the door and left. She hadn't called me Bethy since I was twelve years old.

The rest of the day wasn't nearly as bad (with the glaring exception of the mail, which I forgot to look at until early that evening). We all worked harder and more furiously than usual and at a little after twelve, when we decided to break for lunch, I felt like I had to get out so I offered to take everyone to La Casita on Farwell (very near the house). I needed something to lift my spirits and La Casita always has that effect on me. It's like a mini-vacation to Acapulco. Or maybe Cancún. We stayed for two hours, lazily eating and chatting, trying to forget the morning's events.

Emily was quiet at first, but not in her usual way (aloof and superior). This time it was closer to shyness and humility. After a while, she started to join in the conversation and soon even Mike responded to her in a favorable way. He's an easygoing guy, amiable and friendly with almost anyone, but he and Emily have always showed some hostility toward each other, precipitated for the most part by Emily's rude behavior toward him. But not that afternoon. Both were hesitant and tentative, carefully making just one small gesture of friendliness at a time, until Emily was actually laughing at his jokes, a first from what I could remember. If there's one thing Mike can't resist, it's someone who laughs at his jokes.

That evening, just after Janice and Emily had gone home, Mike started to pack up his things. "What are you doing tonight?" he said.

"Brian and I are having dinner. How about you?"

He shrugged. "Don't know yet. I was just wondering if you wanted to try to reach some of the people from law school about Don."

"Oh, yeah, I forgot all about that," I said. I looked at my watch. "It's early enough. We could probably still reach some of them at work. I can copy some of the pages at the end of the directory and you can do those from this phone while I start at the beginning on the other one."

"How did you learn to be so organized?" he said with complete sincerity.

I stared at him. "Organized? You must be kidding. I'm not organized at all."

"You have to be," he said. "You couldn't do all the things you do if you weren't."

"Mike, I'm telling you, I'm not organized. Look at my desk. This is the one thing Mrs. Gunther doesn't touch. Is this the desk of an organized person?"

He held his breath for a moment, a bit of a wince on his face. "I see your point," he said. "But it's just a desk."

"Mike, this desk is a mirror of my mind."

When he looked at me like I was crazy (I am, but I still don't appreciate the look), I wrinkled my nose at him, took the lawyers' directory to the copy machine, and copied the last fifteen pages of individual lawyer listings. "Here," I said as I handed him the copies. "We might as well get started."

He took them from me and I went upstairs to my second line. It was a lot more work than I expected. I made twenty-seven calls and was about ready to give up when I finally found someone who could help me—my old pal, Sarah Haines.

"Yeah, I heard about the murder," she said. "A bunch of us were just talking about it yesterday."

I asked her who had been present and she told me as I wrote down the names. "The reason I'm calling," I said, "is that I'm trying to locate anyone Don tried to contact in the last several months."

"John Langley said he saw him all the time," she said. "Well, I think it was somewhat sporadic but they definitely kept in touch."

I looked up his name in the directory and read off the firm name and home address that were listed. "Do you know if he's still there?" I asked.

"I don't know where he lives," she said, "but I'm sure he still works for Stroeker."

"Great. Thank you so much, Sarah. You can't imagine how much I appreciate this."

"I'm glad I could help," she said. "Let me know what happens, okay?"

I promised I would and ran downstairs to Mike. He was on the phone, leaving a message for someone named Waupaca.

"Any luck?" I asked him.

"Not yet. How about you?"

"Sarah Haines," I said with a grin. "Remember her? Long blond hair, kind of tall, blue eyes?"

Mike frowned and shook his head.

"Well, anyway, she said she just had lunch with a bunch of people from law school and John Langley was one of them and he said he still saw Don pretty often."

Mike frowned again. "Who's John Langley?" he said.

I looked skyward. "You don't remember anyone."

"I remember you," he said with a teasing smile. "Who else is there?"

I laughed though I tried not to.

"Did you call him?" Mike asked.

"No, I'm going to do it now. I just wanted to come down and tell you first."

"You just wanted to come down and gloat," he said.

John wasn't at his office so I tried the home number listed in the directory. There was no one there, either, and I couldn't leave a message because the phone wasn't picked up by a machine. I let out a sigh and resumed my search. It took fourteen additional fruitless calls before I reached Greg Stetson. But it was well worth the effort.

"Get this," Greg said. "He called about a month ago—no, it was more like three weeks—and he wants a hundred and eighty thousand dollars. Where does he get off asking for that kind of money? And he insists he has to have it by the end of the week but he won't tell me why he needs it. I told him to bug off."

"I think he was in very serious trouble," I said, "and he was getting frantic. He obviously had to raise the money by a particular date and it was beginning to look like he wasn't going to make it."

"Yeah, that fits," Greg said. "He even offered to sign his house over to me but it was just a little too intense for my blood. I have no idea what he was mixed up in but I sure wasn't getting involved."

"Well, I can certainly understand that," I said.

"Jackpot," Mike said when I ran downstairs to tell him the news. His was Walt Yardley, who'd never been friends with Don but whom Don had approached, in his office, asking to borrow five thousand dollars.

"When was this?" I asked.

"He thinks it was sometime in late April or May."

"Interesting," I said. "He asked Greg Stetson for a hundred and eighty thousand within about a week of his death. I think I'm going to have to talk to Glen again, very soon."

I was about to call him when I decided it might be better to pay him a surprise visit just as I had the first time. Monday morning, first thing. I was making a notation in my calendar when I suddenly remembered my mail.

It was the scariest delivery yet. Once again, it involved someone I love, and this time it was someone far less self-reliant than Mike. The photo was of me going into Mrs. Robinson's apartment building the previous Sunday afternoon. The note said *A gOod fRiEnd pERhaPs?* I stared at the floor, willing myself to be calm. "He won't hurt her," I said out loud. "He knows she can't know anything. He knows she's not involved."

When I showed it to Mike he furrowed his brow and asked, "Where is this?"

"Mrs. Robinson's apartment building," I said with a shaky voice.

He looked at me for a moment and I could see the name slowly register by the expression on his face. "Beth, this isn't worth it," he said. "You have to back out."

I gave him a helpless look.

"People are going to get hurt," he said, "including you if you don't watch out. This guy is dangerous, don't you understand that? He's killed at least one person that we know of and he's threatening you and everyone you know."

I sighed and looked away.

"You do recognize that, don't you?"

"Yes, of course I do, but that doesn't mean I have to quit," I said. "It just means I need to keep other people out of it. Maybe I shouldn't see Mrs. Robinson until this is over and maybe you should stay out of it, too. Just let me do it alone. I've done it before."

He leaned back in his chair and grasped his hair with his hands. "Are you out of your mind?" he said. "There's no way I'm going to let you do this alone. If you won't listen to reason I'm just going to have to stay with you until it's over. You got it?" His voice and expression were angry but I knew him well enough to recognize it as love and concern.

"I'm sorry," I said. "I know you're right but I feel obligated now. I can't just give up. People are counting on me to at least try. David's counting on me, if no one else."

"I know," he said. "You're hopelessly stubborn. But it's just one of the things I love about you."

I laughed and he did, too. Then he got up to leave.

"You seeing Andrea tonight?" I said.

He stiffened just a little. "No," he answered quietly. "Not tonight."

I was about to ask him about it but I decided not to. He didn't look like he was in the mood to talk just then.

Brian came at seven and I showed him the photo and the note after a ten-minute hug that felt like heaven.

"Isn't this Grezinski's building?" he said. (Dave Grezinski, Janice's brother who was murdered the year before, had also lived in that building.)

I nodded. "I was going to see Mrs. Robinson. It was last Sunday."

He pursed his lips and tapped the picture against his leg several times. And he talked about it all through dinner.

"I'm not going to waste my breath asking you to stop what you're doing," he said with a sweet but chiding smile, "so I'm going to do the next best thing. I'm going to have to step up the investigation myself."

My immediate reaction was annoyance. I wanted to solve it. I didn't want him stepping up his investigation. The look on my face must have said it all.

"Beth, this is a police matter. I hope you haven't forgotten that," he said.

I glared at him (sort of). "No," I said. "I haven't forgotten." Then I changed the subject, deciding right then and there that I'd just have to step up *my* investigation, too.

THE NEXT DAY was Halloween. The trick-or-treaters would be out in the afternoon and Erma's wake was that night. And of course, I'd forgotten to buy candy. I rushed to the store and picked up what I could find, bought a few other things I really needed (like some food), and went home. I had *two* cartons of yogurt for breakfast, I was so hungry, and then a piece of rye toast. It was either that or a Kit Kat bar and I forced myself to be good at least for the time being.

The afternoon came and went; I ate only three mini Kit Kats and nothing creepy came in the mail. Not such a bad day—so far. I made some homemade vegetable soup for dinner and got ready for Erma's wake. I had a knot in my stomach that got worse by the minute and I was feeling sick. I knew Mrs. Gunther would be in sad shape and I was pretty certain I'd be the one she'd most rely on for comfort. I wasn't sure I could do an adequate job.

The funeral home was way across town and none of us had ever been there, so Mike, Janice, and Emily were coming to my house first, and we were all going in Mike's car (it was the biggest). They were here by six-fifteen and we started on our way in an uncomfortable silence. No one seemed to know what to say. We were painfully conscious of where we were going and we all knew it would be a tough evening. I was glad they were with me, though. It made it easier somehow. Shared discomfort is so much better than discomfort suffered alone. (Now isn't that profound?)

When we walked in, Mrs. Gunther was all alone, sitting on a chair at least three or four feet from the wall. More chairs were lined up against the walls and a number of them had been set up in rows in front of the casket. There was a podium between the casket and the chairs.

At least half a dozen people were in the room but not one was paying the least bit of attention to Mrs. Gunther. I couldn't understand it. Had they already spoken to her and then moved on to pay their respects? I supposed so, but the whole scene looked odd and horribly sad. Mrs. Gunther looked up as she heard us approach and a faint smile brightened her face. I smiled tenderly and gave her a hug. The others did the same, offered the condolences they'd already given but felt obliged to repeat, and then stood awkwardly staring across the room.

"Come on," I said to Mrs. Gunther. "I'll stand with you at the entrance and help you receive people."

She looked up at me with a lost-child face and I held out a hand to help her to her feet. I stayed by her side for the rest of the evening and she introduced me to every guest who came by. The ritual seemed to ease the tension by giving us something to do. Something mindless to focus on. Brian came, stayed for well over an hour, and was very sweet. My parents were there and even my brother Mike, my sister Ann, and her husband Don. I was touched by that, especially by Ann. She's so often caught up in her own world to the exclusion of everyone else's. That night she had tears in her eyes as she put her arms around Mrs. Gunther. Don, whom I find to be almost always obnoxious and self-absorbed, extended his hand, reminded her that they'd met some years back, and said he was very sorry for her loss. His face betrayed a tenderness I hadn't seen before.

When it was over, I asked Mrs. Gunther if she'd like to come to the house for a while, thinking she might not want to be alone. She has no relatives, not even her husband's (he died some years ago and had no surviving family by that time). But she said no, she preferred to be alone. I gave her a long, tight hug and promised to call in the morning.

On the drive home, Janice, Mike, and Emily talked about trick-or-treat and how different it is now from when we were kids. We always went at night when it was creepy and scary, ghosts and goblins threatening to pounce at any moment. Our costumes were handmade by our mothers, and in Mike's case, by his father. I was always a Native American, dressed in a real deerskin outfit (the deerskin was a remnant of my grandfather's hunting hobby) and a black yarn wig made by my mother, who could and still can make absolutely anything. Mike was a pirate every year, with a black patch on one eye, tall black rain boots, a big, blousy white shirt, and a red sash over black pants. Janice's costumes changed from year to year—

she remembered being a ballerina, a bumblebee, a witch, and a ghost. Emily had always been a princess.

Our happy reminiscing left me totally unprepared for what I found as I pulled into my driveway.

TEN

BOTH JANICE AND EMILY screamed and Mike let out something closer to a gasp. I was so frozen with fear that I didn't make a sound. There's a beautiful hundred-year-old oak tree in my front yard. I spent a lot of time in that tree when I was a child, hidden from view in a lush, leafy world, thinking private thoughts and dreaming private dreams. It was a happy place, a haven all my own. But that night it looked sad and tortured. From its lowest limb hung a scarecrow-like form with long brown hair and the word beth painted on its shirt. A rope was tied around the neck and it swung in the wind, back and forth, forward and back, a face with no features, a body with no soul.

Mike jumped out of the car and was about to pull it down when I yelled to him to stop. "I want the police to see it just as it is," I said. He drooped his shoulders and gave me a nod with a sick expression on his face.

I told Janice and Em to go on home (a request to which they readily acceded), grabbed hold of Mike's sleeve, and held on tight. We looked at each other for a few long moments, not saying anything and not needing to.

"Come on," he finally said. "I have a flashlight in my car."

I smiled with gratitude and relief as he put his arm around me and hugged me like a brother. He got the flashlight from his glove compartment and quickly shone it across the entire front portion of my property, then went back and spent more time on places of particular interest, like my front door.

The door is made of solid walnut, recessed in a charming little alcove and surrounded by leaded glass—a true work of art and one of my favorite parts of the house. It had a dagger embedded in its center. When Mike and I looked more closely, we saw that the dagger and part of the door were covered with a red substance which I guessed to be paint but which certainly looked like blood. I shuddered and Mike led me away. There was a sticky substance on my lawn which was hard to see even with the flashlight but it looked like more of the same red paint. We'd gotten it all over our shoes.

The sidewalk, believe it or not, was the most frightening part of all. From one end of my property line to the other, a message was written in large, thick red letters: *TRICK OR TREAT BETH! STAY OUT OF DON'S AFFAIRS OR YOU'LL DIE LIKE THIS.* After the word *"THIS"* was an arrow pointing toward my tree and the swinging "Beth." I know it sounds silly, but at the time I was relieved it hadn't pointed toward the dagger in the door. Then I thought about it some more and I wasn't sure.

As soon as we went inside, I called Brian but he wasn't there so I talked with someone I didn't know. He acted bored and unconcerned.

"We'll send a car over in the morning," he said. "Just leave everything as you found it. We get a lot of this on Halloween. 'Course, it's usually the night before."

"This was definitely not a mischief night sort of prank," I said, trying my best to sound calm and assured rather than hysterical and confused (which he seemed to think I was). "I'm involved in a murder investigation and I'm almost certain that the murderer meant this as a warning to stay out of it."

I could hear him put his hand over the receiver. Then I heard another sound, like that of someone picking up an extension. In a moment, the officer was back on, asked me again to give him my name, address, and phone number, and inquired in some detail about the murder I was involved in and just how I was involved.

"So when will you be over tomorrow?" I asked when I had finished.

"First thing in the morning, ma'am. Eight a.m."

SUNDAY, NOVEMBER 1. I watched out my front window for the police with a cup of tea in my hand. When a man in a squad car pulled up at 8:03, I got a warm jacket from my closet and went out to meet him. He was having a conversation with someone on his radio. Several minutes later, he got out of the car, held out a very large hand, and said, "Sergeant Kowalski, ma'am." He was at least six feet four.

"This ever happen before?" he asked as he waved his hand in a sweeping motion from one end of the damage to another.

"No," I said, sounding surprised at the question. Then I told him what I believed to be the motivation. When he frowned, I said, "It's also the only prank of any sort that was pulled in this neighborhood over the weekend. I think that makes it even more obvious that this was meant to be very personal, not just some random act." I pointed to the hanging figure. "They painted my name on the shirt." Then I pointed to the sidewalk. "And the guy whose murder I'm trying to solve was named Don."

His eyebrows went up and he leaned against his car. "You know McHenry, right?"

I nodded and felt myself blush. He smiled (almost) and began walking around, surveying the damage and the rest of the grounds. I stayed for several minutes, went back inside, and watched him from my front window. When he was finished, he spoke again to someone on his radio and took off. I let out a big sigh, had a warmed-up baking powder biscuit with melted butter for breakfast, and was immediately reminded of Mrs. Robinson. I was supposed to cook dinner for her that night. She was sure to be disappointed if I canceled, but I knew in my heart it wasn't safe for me to see her. I had a lump in my throat when I dialed her number.

"Beth, darling, how are you?" she said. Her voice was so sweet and full of trust, I almost backed down. But I knew I couldn't.

"Mrs. Robinson, I need to talk to you about something very important," I said. "It involves the investigation of Don's murder."

"Yes, dear?" she said.

I took a deep breath. "Someone has been sending me photographs of myself in the mail. It looks like he's been following me everywhere I go and one of the pictures was taken in front of your building when I came to see you last week. I don't want to frighten you but I'm worried about coming to see you again before this case is solved."

I heard an intake of breath and then a deep, sad sigh. "Oh, my dear, I hope you're being careful," she said. "You've told Brian, haven't you?"

"Yes, he knows all about it and he agrees that it would be safer for you if I stayed away for the time being."

"Oh," she said with a moan. "I see."

"I hope you understand," I said. "I'll miss you terribly but I'll call during the week to see how you're doing."

"That would be lovely," she said in a marginally brighter voice. "I'll be waiting for your call."

I smiled and felt close to tears. "I love you, Mrs. Robinson. I'll call you in a few days, I promise."

"I love you, too, dear. 'Bye now."

I sat for a long while thinking of nothing else, feeling sad and frustrated, anxious and then angry. I think it was the anger that gave me the sudden burst of energy. I decided right then and there that I had to get this thing over with as soon as possible. I got my Don file from the library and pored over my notes. Phone calls are faster than face-to-face interviews so that's how I did it.

Elise Jacobs was my first candidate. Still not home, but this time I left a message, vague enough to avoid scaring her away.

David was next. He was home and answered the phone himself.

"David, it's Beth Hartley," I said.

"Beth," he said evenly. "What can I do for you?"

"What do you know about either Don or Glen embezzling money from their clients?"

Silence, then a heavy sigh.

"David, this is really important. Do you know anything about it?"

"It was Glen," he said after a slight pause. "He took the money."

"You're sure it wasn't Don, or both Don and Glen?"

"It's out of the question," he said. "Don had too much integrity. The suggestion is ludicrous."

"Then why did you tell Don that he was going to have to bail himself out of something? What were you talking about?"

Another silence, this one even longer.

"David, Cassandra heard you talking to him on the

phone. When she asked you about it you said Don was having some sort of personal problem.''

''Glen was trying to implicate Don to save his own skin,'' he said after another long pause. ''Don asked me for help and I told him I didn't want to get involved.''

''Did he ask you for money?''

''Why would he ask me for money? He hadn't done anything.''

I was just about to ask about his father's questionable business practices but I decided I might accomplish more if I saved that for later. I said good-bye instead and as soon as I hung up, the phone rang.

It was Elise Jacobs.

''Thank you so much for calling me back,'' I said. Then I explained what I was after.

''I can't talk to you about that,'' she said, and she hung up.

I called her right back and said, ''I already know about the embezzlement.''

''Oh, no,'' she said.

''What I'm wondering is how you found out.''

''I was Mr. Nolte's secretary,'' she said, ''but I was also the firm's bookkeeper. About six months ago, I suspected that money was being taken from the clients' trust funds so I had to say something to Mr. Nolte about it.''

''Is that when he fired you?'' I asked.

''He didn't fire me,'' Elise said. ''I quit. Why would he fire me?''

"I'm not sure," I said. "Are you telling me that you accused your boss of embezzling but that he didn't fire you?" I was nearly certain she hadn't accused Glen but I was interested in the reaction I'd evoke.

"Mr. Nolte?" she said in a screech. "He wasn't the one. It was Mr. Balstrum."

"But how do you know that?" I said.

"Because it had to be him. It was the only explanation."

"Then why did you quit?"

"Because I didn't want to be embroiled in that mess," Elise said. "I wasn't getting myself involved in anything illegal. I have my own reputation to protect."

That I could understand and I said so. "You wouldn't happen to know if that's why Mr. Balstrum and Mr. Nolte stopped talking to each other, would you?"

"That's exactly why," she said. "Each one was accusing the other. It was horrible. I just had to get out of there."

"Well, I don't blame you," I said. "I think I would've done the same thing under the circumstances."

I was about to say good-bye when I remembered Dana. "By the way," I said, "Dana Andrews really wants you to call her. She was kind of hurt by your leaving without saying a word."

Elise let out a small sigh. "I know," she said. "I feel bad about that. I'll give her a call, I promise."

"Thanks, Elise. And thanks for your help."

It was a little after ten on a Sunday morning. What better time to catch people in? I decided to keep going until I ran out of victims. Amy was next on my list.

"Are you making any progress?" she asked after I said hello.

"A little, but I'm hoping you can help me make more."

"I'll do what I can," she said. She sounded a little wary, which put me on my guard.

"Amy, this is really important," I said. "I don't believe you're guilty of killing Don but I do believe you know more than you've told me and I really have to know everything that you know. If you've been holding back to protect someone, that's all the more reason to come forward, especially if the person you're protecting is Don. The only way you can help him now is by helping me solve his murder."

She was silent for a few moments and then I heard her sigh. "You're right," she said. "You're absolutely right. What do you want to know?"

"First of all, why were you at Mr. and Mrs. Balstrum's house with David? Mr. Balstrum said he came home early one day and the two of you were there talking."

Amy sighed again before she began. "This is…well, it's kind of complicated. I don't know if you know anything about this, but Glen Nolte accused

Don of embezzlement sometime back in April. Glen's secretary was the one who put the idea in his head. Don denied it, of course, but then *he* accused Glen. So then Don told David all about it because he didn't know what to do and David wasn't sure if Don was guilty or not. Then about a month before Don was killed, David started getting really worried about him because he was constantly coming to him and begging for money and just acting like he was totally losing it. So David thought I might know something about it. But I really couldn't tell him anything because the first I knew of it was when Don came to me.''

''When was that?'' I said. ''And what did he say?'' I'd already heard Justine's version of the story, of course, but I was particularly interested in whether Amy would tell me the same thing she'd told Justine.

''It was about three months before our divorce,'' Amy said. ''Don said Glen was the one who took the money but that Glen was trying to put the blame on him and he was really worried because it was just his word against Glen's.''

''But why would he tell you about it if you were about to get divorced?''

''Because he was worried it might come out during the divorce. My lawyer was trying to get a share of his law practice for me and Don said that including the practice in the financial settlement would require going over all the firm's books and end up exposing the embezzlement and then he might get blamed for it. He was trying to scare me off and it worked. That

was all I needed to hear. I wasn't
involved in something like that."

"A wise decision," I said. "Did he
thousand dollars to make it?"

Amy paused before she uttered a nearly ina
"Yes."

"Amy, do you think Don was the one who took
the money?"

"I don't know," she said. "I really don't."

"One more question," I said, "on another topic.
Did Don ever mention anything to you about suspecting his father of engaging in some kind of illegal activity in relation to his restaurant business?"

"David asked me about that, too," she said. "I had no idea what he was talking about."

"What did he say? Try to remember it as accurately as you can."

"He asked me if I knew what Don was doing for his dad and what was going on over there, but I couldn't tell him anything. He seemed to think that might be what was making Don so crazy."

"What do you mean?"

"I'm not sure what he was getting at," she said. "I got confused because one minute he'd be talking about the embezzlement and the next he'd be talking about the restaurants. And he kept asking me if I thought Don was afraid of his father."

"Well, I can certainly understand why you were confused," I said. "It doesn't make any sense to me, either."

"If you want my advice," she said, "why don't you just ask David?"

"Yeah, I guess I'll have to. By the way, do you have any idea why he asked you to meet him at his parents' house?"

"He said he had to pick up some papers and it's not too far from where I work so it was a good compromise. I came over during my lunch break."

"Well, that fits," I said. "Thanks a lot, Amy. I really appreciate this. And I have a feeling I may be getting back to you."

"That's fine," she said. "I'm here if you need me."

As soon as we hung up, I scribbled down everything she'd said and read it over a few times. After the third time, I still couldn't make any sense of it so I put it away. It would come sooner or later. It always does.

Number four on my telephone list was Laney Shaw. She was home but couldn't talk. She had company and they were going to be there for a while. I asked her when she might be available and she promised to call me back as soon as her guests left.

That left Cassandra. I was reluctant to call her for fear David would answer the phone but if I waited until the next day, I might not catch her at all, so I decided to take my chances. My luck was with me. David had gone to the office and she was alone in the house. When I told her I had a question for her but that it was a little odd, she laughed and said, "Go ahead, I'm ready."

"Okay," I said. "Is David a photographer? I mean, does he have any special expertise or does he do it as a hobby?"

"Heavens, no," Cassandra said. "The most complicated camera I've seen him use is a 35-millimeter automatic. I'm no better myself, mind you. I don't mean to be critical. It just isn't one of his strong points. Primarily because he never developed any interest, I think."

"I understand," I said. "Thanks, Cassandra. I'll be in touch."

I was making a notation in the file when something awful occurred to me. I called her back.

"Cassandra, it's Beth again. I know this sounds crazy, but how about Don? Was *he* a photographer?"

"You know, come to think of it, he was," she said. "In fact, he took a lot of pictures in Vietnam and actually sold some of them to the news media. I think he was something of an expert."

I drew in my breath and almost forgot to let it out. "But he never taught David anything about it."

"Not that I know of," she said, her patience beginning to sound a bit strained.

"Okay," I said. "Thanks, Cassandra."

I was making a second notation when Laney returned my call.

"Laney, thank you so much for calling me back. I only have a few quick questions for you."

"Okay," she said. Another wary voice, the second one that day.

"Did Don ever talk to you about his partner embezzling money from his law firm?"

"Uh...well, sort of."

"What did he say?"

"That his partner was accusing him and he had to come up with the money."

"But he claimed that his partner was the one who took it?"

"That's what he said."

"Did he say anything about why *he* felt he needed to come up with the money when his partner was the one who was guilty?"

"No, but I did kind of wonder about that," she said.

"Did you ask him about it?"

Laney sighed before she answered. "No, I didn't."

I tried to phrase my next question as discreetly as I could. "Did you have any reason to believe he'd stolen any money from you?" I said.

"No, none at all," she said. "I never would've suspected him of that."

I added a few notes to the file after we hung up and looked at my clock. I'd promised my mom I'd stop by to see her and I was already late. I spent the rest of the afternoon and a good part of the evening there, most of which was filled by a lecture about my lack of common sense, irresponsibility, and immaturity. My mother did most of the talking but even my dad joined in from time to time. When I left I felt immediately relieved but it lasted only a few short moments. From the time I entered my car and all the way home, I had the sense that I was being watched. And followed.

THE NEXT DAY WAS Monday, November 2. The day I planned to visit Glen, once again. But this time I was going alone.

Mrs. Gunther didn't come in and she didn't call. I hadn't expected her to. I called her at home sometime after ten but there was no answer. I spent almost half an hour after that planning my approach with Glen. I had it all worked out by eleven-fifteen and I was just getting ready to leave when my mail came. I had my hand on the mailbox and I drew it back. I didn't want to see it. I didn't want to know. I went into the library, told everyone I was leaving, and headed for Glen's office.

It was raining hard and the sky was so overcast it was nearly dark. When I arrived, I took off my wet coat and told the receptionist that I needed to see Glen immediately, that it was an emergency. She appeared alarmed (I almost smiled) and got him on the line.

"He'll be right out," she said in a stage whisper. I almost smiled again.

When he saw me a big frown swept over his face. "Beth," he said. "What is it? Come on back."

He guided me by the shoulder with a look of genuine concern. When we reached his office, he shut the door, asked me to sit down, and did the same.

"What's happened?" he asked.

"I know about the embezzlement," I said.

His face went pale.

"Do you want to tell me about it?"

He swallowed hard and ran his hand over his face. "Don was taking money from client funds," he said. "I insisted he pay it back and it was more than a hundred and fifty thousand dollars. But he returned it all a couple of months before he was killed."

My eyes were about as wide open as they could be. "He paid it back?" I said. "A couple of months before he was killed?" I just couldn't believe it. "When?" I said. "Do you remember the exact date?"

"It was the end of August. August thirtieth. That was the deadline I gave him." Glen looked at me and frowned. "Why does that come as such a surprise?"

"Because..." I shook my head. "Because I don't know where he would've gotten the money," I said. "And he was going nuts trying to borrow from just about anyone he could think of after he'd already paid you back. It doesn't make any sense. He tried to borrow a hundred and eighty thousand from Greg Stetson a week before he died. Why would he do that if he'd already paid you back?"

Now Glen looked astonished. "I don't know," he said. "Unless he borrowed it from someone to pay me and then had to pay the other person back."

"But then he'd just owe it to a third person. And why was he so frantic about it? It still doesn't make sense." Then I clapped my hand over my mouth. "Oh, no," I said. "Oh, my gosh."

"What?" Glen said with an almost fearful expression.

I breathed in and out a few times. "I can't tell you yet. I have to be sure."

I left without saying good-bye and sat in my car for nearly half an hour, wondering what in the world to do next. I needed to talk to David. And I'd never reached John Langley. I decided to try John first. I found a phone booth in a gas station parking lot and got hold of him at his office.

"John, it's Beth Hartley from law school. I'm helping investigate Don Balstrum's murder and I understand you had some contact with him on a regular basis."

"That's right," he said. "I saw him a couple of times a month. Why? What's the problem?"

"Did he ever mention anything to you about being in any kind of trouble, financial or otherwise, or that he was afraid of someone for any reason?"

"He never said anything like that but he did ask me to lend him some money," John said.

"How much?" I asked.

"Thousands. Well, let me rephrase that. It wasn't a specific request. He said he needed to raise a hundred and fifty thousand over the next several months and he wanted to borrow as much from me as I could afford. I'll tell you, I thought it was asking an awful lot of our friendship.''

I sighed but made sure John couldn't hear it. ''When was this?'' I said.

''In the spring, sometime. Maybe April or May. I can't give you a more precise date.''

''Did you lend him anything?''

''I gave him five hundred dollars,'' John said. ''What was I supposed to do?'' His tone was more than a little grudging.

I sighed again but this time I made sure he did hear it. ''Did he say why he needed it?'' I asked.

''No,'' John said. ''He wouldn't tell me.''

It was well after twelve o'clock and I hadn't eaten since seven so I stopped for some lunch and tried to erase everything from my mind, just for a change of pace. I couldn't do it. No matter what I did to distract myself, *Don, Don, Don* kept running through my head. I finished my coffee, paid the bill, and drove straight to David's office. No warning for him, either.

''How many times did Don ask you for money to pay Glen?'' I asked him after I practically bribed the receptionist and his secretary to let me inside. ''I already know he asked you despite the fact that you've denied it. I just want to know how often.''

David's whole body tensed up. ''At least a dozen times,'' he said through his teeth.

''How much did he ask for?''

''As much as I could spare.''

''Now this is the important part,'' I said. ''When

did he first start asking you and how long did it continue?''

David creased his brow to such an extent that his eyebrows knitted together. Then he shrugged and opened both palms to me, a gesture which unnerved me since it was also one of Don's. ''He started asking in April when Glen accused him and he was still asking up until the day he died.''

''Until the day he died?'' I said. ''You mean you saw him that day?''

''No, but he called that morning. I told him he needed help.''

I scrunched up my face.

''Professional help, I meant. A therapist. I don't know what had gotten in to him but I knew I wasn't the one to help him. He had problems I wasn't equipped to deal with.''

I nodded and watched him carefully. ''Do you know if he asked your father for help?''

David's face went pale. And he didn't answer. When I tried again and still didn't get an answer, I let it go. ''I have another question about your father,'' I said instead. ''I know you suspect him of engaging in something illegal in relation to his restaurants and that you suspected Don of being in on it.''

David's nostrils flared. I was about to continue when he broke in. ''Don wasn't involved but he told me he'd confronted my father about it, which is something no one in my family has ever had the guts to do, I might add. All he wanted from me were damage control suggestions.''

"Damage control suggestions? What sort of damage are you talking about? Are you saying he was afraid of your father?"

"Yes, I'm certain he was," David said. "He'd be crazy not to be. He'd threatened to turn him in to the authorities. No one talks to my father like that and gets away with it. Especially not Don.''.

"You're not suggesting your father killed him, are you?"

David's jaw tensed and he narrowed his eyes. "Of course not," he barked. "It's out of the question."

"One more thing," I said. "Is your father a photographer?"

"No. Why?"

That wasn't the answer I'd expected. "You're sure he's not a photographer?" I said.

David flashed me a look of annoyance. "Of course I'm sure. Why do you ask?"

"I'll tell you later," I said, "when I'm sure myself."

I drove home, made a cup of chamomile tea to relax a bit, and then went for my mail.

Emily walked in the kitchen just in time to witness my reaction. Though she's never been one to offer much in the way of comfort, I was so very glad she was there.

ELEVEN

I DROPPED THE ENVELOPE on the table when I saw what was inside. Emily picked it up.

"This has gone too far," she said after she'd seen the contents. "You're putting everyone you know in danger. You have to stop."

"Forget it," I said. "I'm going to solve it and I'm going to do it today."

She raised an eyebrow.

"Or maybe tomorrow," I said.

That time she smiled.

The photo was taken in front of my parents' house as I was leaving the night before. The note said VIsItinGmOmMy aND dADDY? And there was no postmark. This envelope had not been mailed. It had been hand-placed in my mailbox by the murderer himself. He was getting much too close. But he was also getting reckless, which made me wonder if he might want to get caught.

The only work I had pressing for that week were the two memos I was doing for David. I'd promised him one of them within the next day or two but I was so close to finishing both that I decided to devote the remainder of the day to them and get the job out of the way so I could put all of my effort into solving the murder.

At 11:15 p.m., I was finished. I'd done the editing and final writing on the computer so all I had to do was print the memos and put them in the center of my desk to remind myself to deliver them to David in the morning.

TUESDAY, NOVEMBER 3, the day I solved the case. My prediction to Emily had been accurate after all. I delivered the memos to David first thing in the morning, came back home, and got right to work. I didn't get any scary mail that day, Mrs. Gunther wasn't there, and Mike, Janice, and Emily agreed to leave me alone. I took my Don file to the kitchen, read it once again, and then organized it in a manner I'd never tried before. Dealing with one suspect at a time, I went through every interview and every notation I'd made and wrote down everything that was said either by or about that person so I'd have it all in one place. When I was done, I had a separate file devoted to every person I'd spoken with. Then I made a separate set, this time categorized by topic, and included what each person had told me about a particular matter. Finally, I looked through each file I'd created and made note of any inconsistencies or missing pieces.

I put everything away, took out the yellow pages, and looked for the nearest camera shop. Then I grabbed a notebook, the night photo of my parents' house, and drove to Cordello's on Farwell Avenue.

I showed the photo to the man behind the counter. "This was taken at night, well after dark," I said, "and I'm wondering if you know what sort of camera might be used to take a picture like this."

He looked at it for a few moments, turned it over, and looked at the picture itself once again. "We don't have any in stock but I can order one for you. I have several catalogs I can show you."

I was about to tell him I wasn't interested in buying but I was afraid of losing his attention so I kept that to myself and asked to see the catalogs. He showed me several different models at a wide range of prices. One of the cameras displayed looked awfully familiar and I was pretty sure I remembered where I'd seen one just like it.

"Thanks a lot," I told him. "I'm still shopping around but I may get back to you."

I drove around for at least an hour after I left Cordello's, making circles around the city by moving from I-94 to 894 and back, over and over again. I decided there was only one thing to do, only one way to be sure. I had to get another look at it.

She hesitated before opening the door, though I'd clearly identified myself and gave her no warning of why I was there. I tried my best to look casual and said something stupid like I was just in the neighborhood and thought I'd stop by.

Then I walked to the front window to take a closer look. I'd been right. It was just like the one I'd seen in the catalog. I closed my eyes, took a few deep breaths, and turned around, but by that time she was already pointing the gun at my chest.

"Laney. Why?"

She laughed. "Why?" she said. "How can you even ask?"

I stared at her as I tried to control my breathing and then she started to cry.

"He never loved me," she wailed. "All those months we were together, all those months I waited and waited and he never even cared. He never cared at all."

I tried to give her a sympathetic look. "You told me you were just friends," I said in a soothing voice. "Was it really more than that?"

Tears flowed down her cheeks and her shoulders were shaking. "I thought it was. I thought he left Amy to be with me. I thought he was just waiting. He said it was too soon to be more than friends but I thought he was just waiting. I thought he loved me." Laney let out a sob. "I was so sure we'd be together some day."

I sighed and sat down on the floor. She looked a bit startled but didn't make any move to get me up. "Laney," I said. "What happened? What makes you think he didn't care?"

"He told me," she blurted out. "I asked him if we could go away somewhere for a weekend and he laughed at me. He was so mean about it and I didn't understand so I asked him and he said we were never anything but friends and we never would be and how could I not know that. When I told him how I felt about him, he left me. He *left* me. He wouldn't even let me talk. He just walked out the door.''

"Oh, Laney," I said. "I'm so sorry. I really am."

She looked at me with her brows knit together and then she sank to the floor and leaned her back against the wall.

"When did this happen?" I asked her.

"A week before I killed him," she said with a sigh. She was starting to sound sort of matter-of-fact so I decided to just keep the conversation going and hope for the best.

"Why'd you wait a whole week?" I asked. (What else was I supposed to say?)

She sighed again and started drawing circles on the carpet with the tip of her gun. "I went to see my brother-in-law," she said. "He's a lawyer and I wanted to hire him to do my personal injury case instead of Don but he said he couldn't do it because he's a patent lawyer. But then he asked me all about it and he said Don shouldn't have been doing it, either. He should have referred it, Mark said, but Don actually asked me to give him the case. Mark said that was very unethical. And he was charging me by the hour, too, and Mark said he was only supposed to charge me if he won the case for me, so every penny I paid him he really stole from me. And he wasn't even doing it himself," she added with a burst of anger. "He gave it to *you*."

I was experiencing a pretty strong urge to defend

myself but it really wasn't the right time if you know what I mean. I changed the subject instead.

"How did you learn to take pictures like that?" I asked her.

She waved the gun back and forth. "My father," she said. "He was a professional photographer. He taught me when I was little."

"And that was one of the shared interests between you and Don."

She nodded and I sighed.

"So, where'd you get the gun?" I said next.

That question actually amused her. With a queer little grin on her face, she said, "Don convinced me to get it for protection. Before my divorce was over, my husband was harassing me like crazy. I was scared to death of him. He was following me everywhere so Don got a court order against him but it didn't work so then Don put three deadbolts on my door and made me buy the gun." She laughed a little. "He even paid for the lessons to teach me how to use it."

I closed my eyes and let out another sigh. "So you went to his office to shoot him?" I said.

"No, I went there to scream at him," she nearly screamed at me. "I had just come from seeing Mark and I wanted to tell him what I knew about how he'd been cheating me and stealing from me. But before I could even get out what I wanted to say, do you know what he did? He asked me for money," she said with a expression of horror. "He wanted everything I could afford to give him.'' Her face flushed with the memory.

"He asked me for money," she repeated as she started to sob. "When he did that I just lost it. I pulled the gun out and shot him without even thinking. How could he do that to me?" she cried. "I loved him so much and he never even cared. The whole time we were together I thought he loved me but he never even cared. All he ever did was use me.''

EPILOGUE

LANEY NEVER DID TRY to hurt me. After we'd talked some more, I asked her to put the gun on the floor and push it toward me and she did so without any objection. She kept her head down as I called the police and went with them quietly. On her way out, she looked back at me with tears in her eyes and an expression that pleaded with me to understand. I couldn't find it in me to be unkind, even under the circumstances, so I gave her a small but caring smile.

As often happens when a murder is investigated, some pretty interesting little pieces of information can be unearthed about people who were innocent (of the murder, that is). Art Balstrum was laundering money, as David had suspected, and Don had discovered it while he was still in law school. He actually tried to induce Balstrum to hire him as his attorney—for a very large salary—in exchange for his silence. Balstrum refused so then Don demanded money. Balstrum finally gave in and gave him some part-time work even before he graduated and paid him what he asked, hoping that would suffice to keep him quiet. And it worked (sort of).

Don began embezzling from his clients shortly after he suffered the tremendous loss on the investment he'd made on the basis of Chuck Barker's tip. He apparently believed that Glen would follow through on his threat to turn him in and when he knew he couldn't meet Glen's deadline, he embezzled from his father to pay Glen and took a little extra for spending money (thirty thousand, to be exact).

Don stole the one hundred and eighty thousand from Balstrum in August, paid Glen in full, and then frantically tried to replace it before his father could discover it was gone. But Balstrum found out a month later and quite literally threatened to kill Don if he didn't pay it back. He gave him one month, until October fifteenth. Don was terrified of his father.

I met David at Don's house a few days after Laney was arrested, and we had a long talk. He hadn't known about Don's theft from his father but he'd started to suspect something right before he talked to Amy. At that point, he didn't know what to do. He was afraid for Don but he didn't want to do anything to antagonize his father. After the murder, David actually believed that his father had done it. He hated him for it, of course, but at the same time he was trying to protect him (or more likely, to protect *himself* from the truth) by trying to implicate Glen and Chuck Barker.

He talked for quite some time about his relationship with Don. He knew Don had been treated unfairly all his life and that he was one of the prime instigators. He should have been the one to stop it. To protect his brother rather than berate and humiliate him. He wanted so much to go back and start over again. To do it right. To live his life with some compassion and tolerance. But it was too late. He could never take back the things he'd said, never undo the things he'd done.

He'd been spending substantial amounts of time in Don's house since his death, keeping it clean, repairing little things as he discovered the need. He often felt that Don was there with him, that his presence filled the house, that he was close to him once again. Don left his house to David. David says he'll never give it up.

I had a hard time knowing how to respond to the things he said. So much of it was true. He had treated him badly. It was too late. There wasn't a thing he could do to change the past, so I tried to get him to focus on the future instead. I told him, first of all, that in my experience (which, admittedly, is quite limited) no one is ever happy with the way they've behaved toward someone after that person has died. And it's mostly because we just don't think that way. We don't expect people to die the next day or even the next year. We act, for the most part, as if we'll all be here forever. It's a strange phenomenon given the statistics to the contrary, but it is a fact of life.

And yes, I said, it was true he couldn't relive his time with Don. But what about Cassandra? And his two sons? His mother and his sister? They were still here. He could do for them now what he longed to do for Don.

He got me thinking about my own life and the people I sometimes neglect (including myself). On my way home that morning, I stopped by to visit Mrs. Robinson. She was so happy to see me she got tears in her eyes. I told her it was all over, that everything was all right, and that I'd give her the details later.

"How would you like to go to my mom's house," I said, "and I'll take us all out to lunch?"

She brought both hands to her cheeks with a wide grin and said, "Oh, how lovely." She became so excited I had to sit her down while I got her coat.

Mrs. Robinson had never seen my parents' house, of course, so my mother wanted to give her the full tour which I quietly talked her out of because it would've taken nearly all day if Mrs. Robinson could even manage to survive the journey. She agreed and showed her the living room, the dining room and the kitchen. Then we went to Watt's Tea Room and had a marvelous time. We had lunch and dessert and lots of tea and then went back to Mrs. Robinson's place so she could rest. My mother had never been there either so the day was a real treat for both of them. But I really think I was the one who enjoyed it the most. It felt good to see them so happy, and to know I'd done something to accomplish it. That may sound self-centered, but I don't care. Being good to other people *does* make you feel good about yourself, and for good reason. It's the right thing to do. The best choice to make. Period.

Speaking of which, Emily actually spent last Sunday afternoon with Mrs. Gunther, at Mrs. Gunther's house. She made a pot roast (she's really a good cook) and brought it with her, and they ate and talked until late in the evening. Mrs. Gunther told me all about it the next day. She said it was as if Emily had been transformed. Emily never said a word about it to me. It was her own private kindness, done for the purest of reasons. And she'd done it on her own, without any prompting from anyone.

Amy broke down and sobbed when I told her how David felt about Don. She'd never tried hard enough, either, she said. She should have given the marriage a chance. It might have worked if she'd tried one more time. She'd taken him for granted. She'd never appreciated him, and similar self-deprecating sentiments. I reminded her of what she'd told me: that she'd divorced him because, for both of them, the feelings that had brought them together were gone, and no amount of trying could ever get them back. That calmed her down a bit, but I had to stay with her for quite some time before I was sure she'd be all right. She was nearly hysterical with grief. I had the impression that she'd held it all back until that point. Until she knew exactly what had happened, she hadn't allowed herself to feel the loss.

Mrs. Balstrum could barely speak when Mike and I visited her. I think that she, too, had held back a lot of her grief and she was overwhelmed by it now that it was released. We went back several weeks later and she was feeling a bit better, though. Mike promised

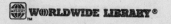

AGATHA AWARD WINNER

JEANNE M. DAMS

KILLING CASSIDY

A DOROTHY MARTIN MYSTERY

Though Dorothy Martin is quite content with her new life in a cozy English village, she looks forward to an unexpected trip back to her Indiana hometown. Sadly, it is the sudden death of a longtime friend and a small inheritance that offer Dorothy this brief holiday in the States.

Along with her inheritance, Dorothy gets a cryptic note from her deceased friend claiming he was murdered. Now, back among the friends and acquaintances of her past, she must find out if one among them is a killer—and why.

"Altogether, this is a warm and worthy read…"
—*Publishers Weekly*

Available November 2001 at your favorite retail outlet.

WJD402

MARY LOGUE

DARK
COULEE

A CLAIRE WATKINS MYSTERY

Though life in rural Wisconsin is having some healing effects for ex-Minneapolis cop Claire Watkins, she is still plagued by nightmares of past tragedy. Now she's plunged into a shattering murder case that will force her to confront the demons that still haunt her.

Widower Jeb Spitzer is knifed to death at the local harvest moon dance, leaving three teenagers orphaned. But Claire senses a feeling of desperate relief among the three kids. As she peels back the layers of the crime, she uncovers a shocking connection to Spitzer's wife's "accidental" death, and secrets that premeditated both incidents.

Available October 2001
at your favorite retail outlet.

MURDER, MAYHEM *And* MISTLETOE

Terence Faherty, Aileen Schumacher, Wendi Lee, Bill Crider

Four new tales of Christmas crimes from four of today's most popular mystery writers.

THE HEADLESS MAGI

What do several alarming calls to a crisis center and vandalism at a local nativity scene have in common? Owen Keane, metaphysical sleuth in Terence Faherty's Edgar-nominated series is about to find out!

CHRISTMAS CACHE

Aileen Schumacher's New Mexico sleuth, Tory Travers, finds herself undertaking a challenging Christmas puzzle: an international network of art thieves, a backyard full of cash, and a mysterious shooting.

STOCKING STUFFER

Wendi Lee's Boston P.I. Angela Matelli uncovers a case of shoplifting that leads to murder…

THE EMPTY MANGER

Bill Crider's easygoing Texas sheriff Dan Rhodes has his hands full with a "living" manger scene in downtown Clearview, especially when the body of the local councilwoman is found dead behind it.

Available November 2001
at your favorite retail outlet.

 W⊕RLDWIDE LIBRARY®

I have to go see Andrea.'' Then he gave me a big hug and left. As of yesterday, they're still talking and still fighting. But Mike looks so much happier.

Since we're on the topic of romance, I guess I should say something about Brian. He's *wonderful*. He's *the best*. He was so proud of me when I solved the case that he actually brought me to the station and introduced me to everyone. And they had a little surprise party for me with coffee and a big cake. It was so sweet, I couldn't believe it. Something I'll never forget as long as I live. Another gesture of kindness and love, for all the right reasons.

her we'd come to visit every month and she hugged him for nearly a minute.

Mike and I finally talked about what had been bothering him. Andrea broke up with him because she said he ignored her too much and never paid any attention to her needs.

"You know what I think?" I said.

He looked at me with eyes full of trust.

"I think maybe the two of you just have a problem communicating. Maybe you just need to sit down and talk about what each of you wants and how you feel."

He cringed and I smiled.

"I know that sounds kind of scary," I said, "but as far as I'm concerned, it's the only way to have a relationship. How can you be happy and content with someone if you can't talk about how you feel? You don't need to do it all at once, you know. Just start slowly. Just one tiny conversation at a time. But tell her you want to talk, and tell her it's hard for you. Then maybe she'll be patient and understanding about it."

Mike rubbed his face with such aggression I was afraid he'd hurt himself. Then he put his head on the table and groaned. I touched his shoulder and got up to make us some tea. Before I had finished, he went to the phone and called Andrea. I couldn't hear her end of the conversation, of course, but he asked her if she'd like to talk and he had a huge grin on his face when he hung up.

When I held out his cup of tea, he said, "I can't.